Country Girl, City Girl

LISA JAHN-CLOUGH

Houghton Mifflin Company Boston 2004

Walter Lorraine (wʀ) Books

For Elena, Eric, and Garrett

Walter Lorraine (wL) Books

Copyright © 2004 by Lisa Jahn-Clough

www.houghtonmifflinbooks.com

Library of Congress Cataloging-in-Publication Data

Jahn-Clough, Lisa.
  Country girl, city girl / Lisa Jahn-Clough.
    p. cm.
  "Walter Lorraine Books."
  Summary: When thirteen-year-old Melita, the sophisticated daughter
of a New York actress, comes to visit Phoebe, who has been raised by
her father on a farm in Maine, Phoebe discovers she has confusing
feelings about their developing friendship.
  ISBN 0-618-44791-1
  [1. Interpersonal relations—Fiction. 2. Identity—Fiction. 3. Farm
life—Maine—Fiction. 4. City and town life—New York (State)—New
York—Fiction. 5. Mothers—Fiction. 6. Maine—Fiction. 7. New York
(N.Y.)—Fiction.] I. Title.
  PZ7.J153536Co 2004
  [Fic]—dc22

                                          2004000733

Printed in the United States of America
MP 10 9 8 7 6 5 4 3 2 1

ACKNOWLEDGMENTS

With good fortune, behind every writer there are a few helpful people. I am grateful to those who have offered their support, encouragement, and criticism along the way: Pam Richards, Jack Gantos, Jenefer Shute, Fiona McCrae, Anne Hoppe, Mike Demers, Marion Dane Bauer, Kenny Cournoyer, Mitch Levine, Liza Ketchum, Amy Rose, Matt Spowart, Kyle, Sophie, and Bella, my wonderful friends and family, my brilliant colleagues, and all my amazing students, former and current. A special thanks to the good people at Houghton, especially Walter Lorraine, editor extraordinaire, and Stacy Graham, assistant extraordinaire. And, of course, to my darling four-legged companions: Gracie, who keeps my printer warm, and Happy who always listens, unless there is something more interesting in the garbage.

Country Girl,
City Girl

Country

1

I unlatched the wooden gate of the goat pasture and headed to my favorite sitting rock. Petunia waddled over, chewing her cud.

"Ready?" I said, stroking her fur and jingling the bell on her collar. "We're reading a new story today. You'll like it. It's about a girl who falls asleep for one hundred years." I took the worn copy of *Grimm's Fairy Tales* from under my arm. It was the same copy I'd had all my life, the one Dad used to read to me at bedtime when I was little. Even though I had just finished seventh grade, I still loved old fairy tales. When Petunia gave birth, I planned to read to her kid, too. By the size of her belly, it looked like, once again, she had more than one in there. Last year Petunia had twins, and I gave them English and history lessons so that by the time we sold them they were the smartest goats in Maine.

Every year we take Petunia to a farm in the next town to breed her with a buck. I used to go along and watch them prance around in what Dad calls their mating ritual. The buck lunges after Petunia, who always skitters away, until finally she lets him climb on her back. The last time I went I felt sorry for Petunia. It didn't look as though she was having much fun. If that's all there is to sex, it's never going to be for me. It's probably unfair to compare goats to humans, but after all, we're animals, too.

This spring I told my father I didn't want to go anymore. He was disappointed. He thinks it's good for my brother, Phil, and me to be educated about nature. But I wanted to give Petunia some privacy. It seemed like the more I knew about that sort of stuff the less I wanted to think about it. Kids in school had already started dating and doing things I didn't want anything to do with. Not to mention that they didn't want anything to do with me, either.

I cleared my throat and began reading. "Sleeping Beauty. By the Brothers Grimm. Read by Phoebe Sharp." I glanced at Petunia. She continued chewing. "Once upon a time, in a far-off land, there lived a couple who longed for a child." I managed to finish half the story before Petunia tried eating the pages.

"Hey! None of that. Don't you like it?" I held the book out of reach. "That's it for today, anyway. It's suppertime." I led Petunia into the barn and scooped some grain into her bin. She ate eagerly and ignored me when I tried to give her a hug.

"See you tomorrow for morning milking," I said.

I took out my camera, a crappy Instamatic I got at a yard sale last year, and clicked the end of my roll on Petunia. I was marking the progress of her pregnancy. Someday I would have a real camera. A 35 mm with a zoom lens. How could I be a professional without a zoom lens? While I was at it, I would have my own darkroom, too. Instead of piling up rolls and rolls of film waiting to

2

be developed, I could print my own and make artistic changes in light and focus. Watch the image emerge right before my eyes in a deep red glow. The problem was money. Dad works but there's not much extra. I'm pretty good at saving my baby-sitting money, but photo equipment costs a lot, and in our tiny town there's limited baby-sitting to be found.

Most of my photos were of the animals and the farm and always in black and white. I should have lived in the era when photography was new because I love all that old equipment, the old box cameras, which had a black cloth that you hid under in order to take a picture. But for now I had to be satisfied with photography books from the library and my own Instamatic.

On my way down the path I stopped by the stone wall and took a deep breath. Our black lab, Bear, ran up to join me. We stood there, both breathing in with our noses held high. The air smelled of new leaves. I wrapped my arms around myself and watched the misty pink sun begin to drop over the hills. The days were getting longer, and it was lighter later. It was still a little chilly in the evenings, but it was feeling almost like summer. I loved this time of year. It was fresh and untouched, as if anything could happen. It was romantic, like a fairy tale. I sighed and then headed inside with Bear jumping and barking at my heels.

As soon as I walked into the kitchen, Dad hung up the phone. He let out a big sigh. "Well," he said.

"Well, what?" I asked.

"We'll discuss it after dinner. Now help your brother set the table."

My dad. He tries his best, but I don't think he's ever

3

recovered from my mother's death, almost eleven years ago. He's not bad looking, especially if he shaved off his beard, but he's hardly ever dated in my entire lifetime. About five years ago, he went out with the school librarian for a couple of dinners. He put on a tie and hired Michael to watch us, but then all of a sudden he stopped calling her. When I asked him about it, all he said was that she wasn't for him and that was that. You'd think he'd want to find someone to keep him company, but the way he's so quiet and stern would probably drive any woman away. I wonder if he was like this when my mom was alive, or if he developed this stiffness after. Before my mom died he was going to go back to school to get his degree in biology, but now he works for our neighbors who run an organic seed farm. It gives him enough time for our farm and allows him to keep an eye on Phil and me, though it's mostly me he's strict with. Phil gets away with murder, probably because he's older and a boy.

Some people might wonder why we don't sell the farm and buy a place in town, but that would devastate my dad almost as much as losing my mother did. I'm just as glad, because it would devastate me, too. I love this farm and wouldn't want to ever live anywhere else. I was born here. I know all the paths through the woods and which rocks they lead to, I've seen the trees grow, and every night the sunset is different. The only thing that would get me to leave is studying photography with one of the masters, like Ansel Adams or that guy who took photos of still lifes of fruit and made them look like landscapes. Too bad they're dead. Like I said, I should have been born in a different era.

All through dinner, Phil went on about Crystal, his newest girlfriend—how cool and pretty she was, how she liked him. Phil is the opposite of me. He's popular. Everyone thinks he's good-looking, he always has a girlfriend, he's smart without being too smart, and no one ever makes fun of him for being arty or too quiet. Phil and I used to play all the time when we were little kids, but ever since he started high school, we've drifted in different directions. Now he was excited about his last year of school while I was dreading eighth grade. I wished I could be almost out for good. Summer was, by far, my favorite season. No school.

I was quiet through dinner. Not unusual for me. When we were done, Phil got ready to excuse himself.

"Just a sec," Dad said, scratching his beard. "There's something we need to discuss."

"A family discussion?" Phil groaned. "I told Crystal I'd call her."

"This involves us all. You can call her after," Dad said.

"What is it?" I asked, taking a sip of water.

"I got a call from an old friend from college," Dad said. "A close friend of your mother's."

Phil stopped fiddling with his fork, and I put my glass down with a *kachink*. Dad hardly ever mentioned our mother. I was only two when she died of cancer, so I don't remember her at all. She used to be a designer; she made clothes and sets for the theater and stuff, but she gave it up to have kids and raise them on a farm. Phil says he remembers Halloween, when she sewed our costumes by hand. One year he went as a dog and I went as a turtle. She made the shell out of wire and soft fabric.

5

"This woman was your mom's best friend at NYU. Her name is Gerelyn. She's an actress. She has a daughter." He paused and we waited for more. "Gerelyn did okay after college. Moved to Los Angeles and got a few bit roles in movies, and she was in some commercials. She made good money. She got commercial jobs for the baby, too." I had never heard anything about this friend. My mother, and father, too, knew a real actress? Why hadn't he ever mentioned this? "She's living back in New York City now. She's having a hard time."

"Dad, I'm glad you had friends and all, but Crystal's waiting. Can I go?" Phil asked.

"Just a minute, Phil." Dad took a breath. "Gerelyn needs some help and is going to check herself into a clinic for a couple of months. She battles with pretty severe depression."

No one said a word. Everyone gets depressed nowadays, but to go to a clinic for it, that's pretty serious.

"I think she may have attempted suicide," Dad said, barely above a whisper.

"Oh, geez. That's bad," Phil said.

"Yes, it is. And it's why we should help her out. She was a good friend to your mother."

"I don't get how this involves us." Phil edged back in his seat.

"She lost touch with us after a while. But she turned up for the funeral, toddler in tow." Dad seemed to be talking more to himself than to us. He rubbed his face with his hands and continued, "Well, the gist of it is, Gerelyn is going to go to a clinic this summer and needs a place for her daughter to stay."

"Here?" said Phil. "She's going to stay here?"

"Well, it might be a good thing. She's close to Phoebe's age. She could help on the farm, keep you kids company."

"I've got Crystal to keep me company," Phil said. "Unless she's cute."

I shot Phil a look.

"What?" he said. "There's no harm in looking."

"Whether she's cute or not, it's something I want us to consider. It would be a huge help to Gerelyn, and I'd like to help her."

"What's the daughter's name?" Phil asked.

"Melita," Dad said.

Phil burst out laughing. "Like the coffee?"

"I suppose so," Dad said. "I remember she was an unusual baby. Very striking."

"Where would she stay?" I asked, fearing the answer. My mind was trying to grasp the idea of someone else being around. I didn't like it. I also didn't like what I thought Dad was going to say.

"She could sleep in the guest room," he said.

"That's my workroom!" I groaned. It was true. Sort of. I kept my photographs in there and some art supplies in case I ever wanted to do something creative. I hoped someday it would be my darkroom. But I hadn't used it all year. Just clicked my crappy camera and collected rolls of film.

"You can work in your bedroom for a summer, Phoebe. It'll be good for you to have someone your age around," Dad said. This meant he had already made up his mind. "You need more friends," he added. Dad is always telling me I need friends. But I disagree. I have the goats. I have my books. I have my art. But most of all I have my mind, which, as far as I can tell, is more imaginative than any of my fellow classmates' in all of Plattville. Not that there are very many—twenty-two in my entire year. In the fall we would all start at the fancy new consolidated school in Dunham, where kids would be bused in from all over. It was a bigger school, but not necessarily better.

"Let's make this work, kids," Dad said. "The point is that we'll have another person around for the summer. The poor kid probably needs some stability in her life." Dad loved taking care of things. That was the whole idea behind living on the farm. He could take care of the animals. But a person was different. "So what do you think?" He lifted his eyebrows in a question that was already answered.

"Why not?" Phil said. "I'll be hanging with Crystal most of the time anyway."

"Phoebe?"

No! I wanted to scream. *I have big plans this summer. Of course I don't exactly know what they are yet, but they certainly don't involve some crazy person's kid named after coffee being in the way!* But I shrugged my shoulders. "I guess," I said.

There went everything. Down the drain.

2

The more I thought about it, the more I decided I definitely wouldn't like Melita. And then I saw her. Dad went to pick her up at the bus station. I opted to stay home and read. But when the car pulled up, I stood in the doorway and watched. Stared is more like it. Melita stepped slowly out of the car, not timid at all, more as if she were disgusted. Bear came loping over and jumped on her. She screamed. Dad dragged him off and scolded him, apologizing to Melita.

Melita stooped to gather her luggage, then stood straight. She was tall and curvy. There *was* something striking about her. Her skin was silky tan, like coffee with extra cream, and I wondered if that's why her mother named her what she did. Her cropped hair, jet black and crunchy with gel, had a bright purple streak running down the middle and was held back with a sparkly barrette. Her nose stuck out at a peculiar angle, giving her face a distinct nonperfect perfection. Her eyes moved around slowly taking it all in. I didn't usually like taking pictures of people, but I wanted to capture her on film.

She wore a sheer black T-shirt you could see her bra through, and she had enough there to need one. Her jeans hung so low on her hips her bellybutton was able to catch flies. On her feet was a pair of black criss-cross sandals with a fat platform heel that made her look even taller than she was. A few kids in school would have liked to dress like her, but their style didn't even come close. Not that there is anywhere near Plattville where you could buy stuff like that. The closest mall was hours away, and that was no fashion mecca.

I could tell Melita was sizing me up at the same time. Probably seeing my crazy hair unraveling from its corkscrew braids, my tiny pig nose covered in freckles, my nonexistent eyelashes, and my tiny chest. And wouldn't you know it, I hadn't had time to change like I'd planned, and I was still wearing my overalls with a big grease stain on the front.

"Phoebe," Dad said. "Why don't you show Melita around the place? Make her feel at home."

I glared at him, then turned to Melita all smiley. Her lips were colored with a dark mauve shade of lip-gloss and pursed together tightly as if she were trying not to breathe. I'd show her what the rugged life was like.

"You want to see the sheep?" I asked.

"Sheep?" Melita said, dropping her suitcase in the entryway. Dad passed us with the rest of her bags, three in all.

"You might want to change your shoes." I held up a ratty pair of sneakers. "Here. These should do." I looked at her feet. Her toenails were painted bright gold. I could just make out a dark mark on her ankle like a smudged tattoo. It looked like some sort of bug, a butterfly maybe, about the size of a grape.

She sneered at the sneakers, but I could tell she was trying to be polite. "That's all right. I'll wear what I have," she said.

"You'll have to step in dirt and poop and everything," I said.

She reached for the sneakers, then hesitated. She rubbed the tattoo. It looked like it was done in Magic Marker.

"Just wear them." I smiled, and to my surprise she smiled back and put them on, leaving her pretty sandals on the bench under the coat rack. The funny thing was, the ratty old sneakers looked great on her.

On the way to the sheep, we passed the goat's pen.

"This is Petunia," I said, stroking Petunia's neck through the fence. "She's going to give birth any day now. She's so fat she'll probably have twins. She had twins last year. Two girls. That's good. You don't want to have boy kids because they're harder to sell."

"How come?"

"Boy goats aren't good for anything except breeding. Females can always give milk. They're good luck, too."

I opened the gate and motioned for Melita to follow me. She did, but looked ready to bolt if necessary.

"You can pat her," I said.

"She won't bite? I thought goats eat anything."

"They only nibble, really. Petunia's the friendliest goat in the world. Right, Petunia?" I put my arms around Petunia's neck and hugged her. Petunia nibbled at my hair. "Oww." I laughed as I pulled it out of her mouth. "See?" I said to Melita.

Melita cautiously reached out her long, thin arm and patted Petunia between her pointed ears. She patted up

11

and down, more like a tap than a pat. I can always tell how comfortable people are with animals by the way they touch them. The way Melita was tap-tapping on Petunia's head meant that she didn't trust animals. But after all, Melita was from the city and had probably never even seen a goat before.

"Nice goat. Nice Petunia," Melita said. Petunia blinked every time Melita's hand came down on her head. "She's not as soft as I thought."

"Try her neck. Like this." I took Melita's hand and put it on Petunia's warm neck and then ran it across her back. I let go, and Melita kept her hand there, perched.

"Soft," she said.

"Feel her belly," I said. "Sometimes you can feel the babies kick." We put our hands on Petunia's fat belly and kept them still, waiting for a sign of life. I held my breath.

"I can't feel anything," Melita said.

"Shh," I said, as if we might wake them. "Just wait." We waited.

"There!" I said. "Did you feel that?"

"No."

"It was there. It kicked. You didn't feel it?"

"I didn't feel anything."

"That's too bad. Maybe you'll be here when she gives birth."

"See them actually come out?" Melita said.

"Yeah, it's cool to watch. Gross, too. Last year, she had them at three in the morning. Dad woke me up and made me come out to the barn."

"I'd like to see a birth." Her hand was still perched on

Petunia's belly as if she was expecting the kids to come out any second.

"Come on. Let's go to the sheep," I said.

I don't know why I was so chatty with Melita. I guess I wanted to prove that just because I lived on a farm and had never been to California or New York, or even out of the state, I wasn't stupid. But I wasn't about to admit that I read fairy tales to the goat.

As we were heading out the back of the barn, I heard the rattle of the familiar red truck pull up the driveway.

"It's Michael!" I said and immediately turned back.

"Who's Michael?" Melita asked, following.

"He helps Dad with some of the farm stuff." Secretly I thought of Michael as my prince, my knight in shining armor, who would someday recognize my unseen beauty and we would live happily ever after. I know he thought of me as a kid, but in five years, when I was eighteen and he was tweny-five, the age difference wouldn't be such a big deal. Most fairy tale girls were teenagers when they married. Not to mention pioneer times, when girls would marry at thirteen.

"Come on." I darted through the barn, past Petunia, and through the swinging gate to the driveway where Michael was stepping out of his truck.

"Hey Phoebe-Dweebie!"

I smiled. When Phil or anyone at school called me Phoebe-Dweebie or Phoeb-the-Dweeb, I wanted to pound him to a pulp, but the way Michael said it just made me smile, and I felt the warmth rush to my face. Anything he called me was okay as far as I was concerned.

13

"Who's your pretty friend? Not from around here, eh?" he asked.

It hadn't occurred to me that Michael would think Melita was pretty. But of course she was. Did he want to touch her hair, too?

I also realized that although Michael called me a lot of things, he never called me pretty. No. *Cute* seemed to be my word. Cute like a rabbit.

"Aren't you going to introduce us, Phoebe?" Michael asked.

"Uh. This is Melita Forester. She's here for the summer."

Michael stuck out his hand and said, "Very charmed to make your acquaintance, Melita. The name's Michael. At your service." And he did a little bow. "That's a lovely name. Melita. Where are you from?"

"All over," Melita said. "I was born in LA, moved to New York when I was a baby, then New Mexico for a little bit, we were in London for a year, and now back in New York."

"Wow," Michael and I exclaimed at the same time. I noticed that Michael was still holding her hand, and Melita didn't seem to mind.

"But now I guess I live in Maine." She said "Maine" like it was a word with dirt on it.

"Aw, it's not so bad here. And you're in good hands. Phoebe knows this place inside out. Though I bet this farm and small town must seem awfully puny to you, huh?" He finally let go of her hand and winked at me. In spite of myself, I grinned.

"It's okay. I patted the goat." Was there a slight hint of soft pink on Melita's cheeks?

14

"Never a dull moment around here, right, Phoebe? You gonna be in the same class as Phoebe when school starts?"

"Oh, I'll be back in New York by then," Melita said. "This is only temporary. Besides, I'm older than Phoebe."

"You look older. What're you? Sixteen?" Michael raised his eyebrows and ran his hand through his curls.

"Fourteen. I'm starting high school in the fall."

"Where are your parents?"

Melita haphazardly kicked the dirt with her foot. "My father's out of the picture. He lives in Sicily. And Mom" —she paused—"she's on vacation."

"What is this? Twenty questions?" I butted in. I wanted to save Melita from questions about her mother, or her father for that matter. Maybe introducing Melita to Michael wasn't such a great idea after all. "We're on our way to see the sheep."

"Hey, that's always fun," Michael said. "A good look at Lambchops and Patty before they end up in the freezer. I'll be in the barn brushing Star, if you girls want to hang out later."

I mumbled something like uh-uh, then headed to the sheep pasture as Michael began unloading some stuff from his truck.

"Isn't Michael great?" I said, feeling Melita out.

"He's all right. He asks a lot of questions." She shrugged.

Melita kept walking, and I tried to read her face to see if she was pretending not to care. Her expression looked exactly the same. Blank.

The sheep were at the far side of their pasture. We keep

15

them out there during the day and in a stall next to Petunia at night. The sheep are never considered pets because we buy two every year and keep them only a few months before they are slaughtered. I try not to get too attached, like I do with the goats. When it comes time for Dad to take the shotgun into the pasture, I hide in the old hayloft at the top of the barn with a pillow over my head, but still the sound of gunfire echoes all over the farm. It doesn't bother me so much once they're dead, but the killing is not something I ever want to watch.

I unlatched the wire fence and we walked in.

"What are their names?" Melita asked.

"Lambchops and Patty."

Melita laughed. "You mean Michael wasn't joking? Those are really their names?"

"Yup. We always name them that, just so we don't forget what they're here for."

"You really eat them?"

"Sure. What did you think?"

"I don't know. It just seems so sad. You don't"—she paused—"you don't eat the goats, too, do you?"

"Of course we don't eat the goats! How could you even think of such a thing? Petunia gives us milk. We drink that. You eat meat, right?"

"Yeah."

"Well, you just buy yours in the store and you don't see where it comes from. That meat was once a cow or a pig or a sheep. It's the same thing." I tried to make it sound like it was no big deal, and usually it wasn't. It was just a part of the farm. How could I explain this to Melita when just looking at her pretty face made me feel ugly?

Lambchops and Patty sauntered over. Lambchops was slightly bigger and had a black muzzle, but otherwise they looked the same.

"What's the matter with this one's tail?" Melita pointed to Lambchops, who had his rear end toward us. I put my hand on his back, and he skidded a few feet away.

An elastic was wrapped around the base of his tail. My father had put it there because the tails get dirty and gross and there is no way the sheep can clean itself. Eventually the blood stops circulating and the tail falls off, making it easier and more comfortable for the sheep. I don't know why Dad bothered doing this, since we eat the sheep anyway. Maybe it was just courtesy. I told this to Melita. Her face scrunched up like she was going to puke.

I bent down to pull Lambchops's little tail to show her. As I lifted the tail up, Lambchops ran off. I looked at my hand. Clutched between my fingers was the tail, a fluffy, gray thing sodden with poop and urine.

Melita let out a scream and then said, "Gross, gross, gross," over and over.

I was stunned for a second, then burst out laughing. "That's what's supposed to happen. It doesn't hurt him. It's like Eeyore. Now we get a tack and just tack it back on." I thought that was pretty funny, but Melita just stared at the tail.

"That is totally and utterly gross," she said.

"I suppose, if you aren't used to things like this," I said. The tail, which looked like a piece of dirty cotton, hung limp in my hand.

I remember when I first found out about this rubber-band technique. Dad explained to me about cutting off the circulation slowly so the sheep didn't feel anything. He told me the same thing would happen if I wrapped an elastic around my finger. I wanted to see if he was right, so I tried it on my thumb. I wound the rubber band so tight that in less than a minute my thumb turned from red to purple to blue. I panicked and took it off. Then I tried it on one of my braids and left it there until bath time came and we had to cut the elastic to get it off, but my braid was still intact.

"Can we go back?" Melita asked.

"Sure. Here, do you want this?" I dangled the smelly tail in front of Melita's pretty face. She shirked away.

"Uh, no. No thanks."

I tossed the tail on the ground. It lay there, barely noticeable, a dirty spot in the tall grass.

"You're just going to leave it there?" Melita said, bending down and moving the grass away to expose the tail. "Maybe we could use it for something."

"Take it then," I challenged her. To my surprise she reached out to pick it up. Was she actually going to touch it? Maybe she wasn't as chicken as I thought. But before her fingers could grasp the fluff, she drew her hand away.

"I can't. You do it."

I picked up the tail, wiped it in the grass, and put it in my jeans pocket. I smiled at her. She smiled back.

"Let's go, " I said and latched the fence behind us.

3

Melita asked questions all through dinner. How much land did we own? How many animals did we have total? Did we eat the chickens or just their eggs? She didn't hold back on anything. Phil answered her with some exaggeration (we owned all the land she could see around us, we ate the chickens that misbehaved), and Dad corrected him with the facts (we had five acres, we ate the chickens after the new ones were old enough to produce eggs). I just watched them all like they were a sad comedy act.

Melita seemed totally comfortable. You'd think she'd be freaked out, being dropped off without knowing anything about us while her mother was in a clinic, but if she was nervous or self-conscious, she didn't show it. She fit in better at the dinner table than I did.

"So are we, like, eating one of your animals right now?" she asked, biting into a slice of lamb.

"Oh, Patty!" Phil exclaimed, shaking his head sorrowfully and examining the meat on his plate. "She was one of the best."

"We slaughter the sheep and some of the chickens for meat," Dad said, ignoring Phil.

Melita nodded as if she knew all about it.

"Everyone around here is expected to do some chore," Dad began. *Uh-oh, here it comes,* I thought. *Dad's chore speech.* "A farm is run by everyone who lives on it, and so while you're here, Melita, you'll have a job to do, just like Phoebe and Phil."

Melita's eyes opened from almonds into wide ovals. She had very expressive eyes.

"Don't worry, it won't be anything you can't handle. Phoebe milks and feeds the goat. Phil does the sheep and chickens. But now that you're here, I can use Phil for some other help this summer and you can take over the chickens. How about that?" He made it sound like he was awarding her a prize and not a chore.

"Okay," Melita said. If there's one thing about my father, he's very hard to say no to.

"Phil will take you through it. It's not hard. You'll love the chickens," Dad said. "And there's nothing like a fresh, organic egg."

"You have to watch out for Colorful," Phil warned. "He's one ornery rooster. He likes to attack strangers." Phil was only half joking. Colorful had a stunning array of orange, red, and brown feathers, but he was very protective of the roost. Occasionally he would lunge after random people who came into the chicken coop, squawking and cackling at the top of his lungs, fluffing out his feathers, and coming straight at them with his claws out. "I take the pitchfork in with me to fend him off," Phil said.

"Don't worry," I told Melita when I saw the look of horror on her face. "Colorful only goes after boys. He never does that to me."

Melita smiled but didn't seem convinced.

I started to feel a little sorry for her.

After dinner, Dad carried Melita's bags upstairs to the guest room, my workroom. "This is your room now, Melita. Phoebe will move the rest of her stuff." I had already cleaned out my photos and material, but there were still some piles of books in the corner. "Well, I'm sure you two want to get a little better acquainted, so I'll leave you. And welcome to our home, Melita." He left the door open and went back downstairs.

"Is he always so formal?" Melita asked.

I'm used to Dad, but seeing him through another person's eyes could make him seem kind of strict. He liked to run a tight ship, as he was fond of saying.

"It's just how he is," I said.

"Sure, that's okay. I wasn't complaining or anything. I know how to handle his type." Melita started unpacking. She unzipped one bag and began to put an array of toiletries on the bookshelf.

"What's all that for?" I asked.

She held up a slender white tube. "This is facial scrub." She picked up a green glass bottle. "This is astringent for after washing." She put those down and picked up a small round jar of white cream. "This is lotion with SPF 15 in it for the sun. Not that I need it, but Mom insists. This other jar is nighttime cream, and these are all my lipsticks." She pointed to a clear plastic zipper bag full of tubes, which she dumped out and began sorting. "So what do you want to be when you grow up?" Melita asked.

"I don't know," I said.

"You must have an idea, at least."

I shrugged. "What about you?" I asked.

"A model. Either that or a psychologist. I guess if I can't make it as a model, I'll be the shrink."

"Oh," I said, thinking of her mother. "Weren't you in commercials?"

"A long time ago. I can't really remember it. I have some pictures."

"Do you look like your mother or your father?"

"I never met my father. Mom wanted a baby, not a husband. She met him in Sicily when she was filming a commercial. He sends a birthday card if he remembers."

"Oh," I said.

"I've seen a picture of him, though. He's your classic tall, dark, and handsome Sicilian guy. Someday I'll go over there and meet him. Maybe even live with him. He owns a vineyard."

"Oh," I said again.

"He's why my skin's so dark. The one thing I got from him. I always have a good tan." She held out her arm and rotated it to expose the creamy brown underside. "My mom's skin is white, white, white. She keeps out of the sun all the time. It freaks her out just to look at the sun. I don't know how she ever lived in California. But she must have looked cool next to someone with such dark skin."

I didn't know what to say to that.

"Does that bother you?" she asked.

"No," I said quickly. "Why should it bother me?"

"Well, you just made a funny face."

"I was looking at your skin," I said. I was also thinking how beautiful it was, smooth, like silk, and a color like,

22

like . . . "Caramel," I blurted out. "You're the color of caramel."

Melita snorted. "You're right," she said, with a touch of sarcasm. "And you're the color of a peach."

I turned the color of a tomato.

"My mom's never been married, but she's had lots of boyfriends of all different ethnicities," Melita said.

I think she was trying to shock me. Maybe she was trying to get back at me for Lambchops's tail. I couldn't blame her really. But I couldn't be shocked easily.

"That's cool," I said, though I was uncomfortable talking about her mom. I didn't exactly know what had happened to make her try to kill herself, but it must have been something serious. Maybe she was an alcoholic or took drugs. Maybe having all those boyfriends and not believing in marriage did something to you.

"She had a long-term boyfriend when we lived in New Mexico. She moved there for him. But it didn't last. Nothing lasts forever."

"Oh." I was beginning to feel like an "oh" machine, but I didn't want to say the wrong thing.

Melita fingered her tattoo. She grabbed a Sharpie marker from the desk and began tracing over it. "I'm going to get a real tattoo as soon as I'm old enough. Maybe on my fifteenth birthday. There's a place in the East Village that doesn't even check how old you are," she said. "A butterfly just like this. And maybe a skull and crossbones right above my butt." She lowered her jeans a little. "Right about here." She touched her back with the marker to make a spot. Dad wouldn't even let me get my

23

ears pierced, let alone a tattoo.

"So are you into photography or something?" Melita asked, pointing to my books. I was happy she changed the subject.

"Yah, I guess. I want to be a photographer. Or an artist." I picked up the book on landscapes of the West.

"A photographer is an artist."

"I know."

"Do you take your own pictures?"

"Some."

"Let me see."

"I don't have very many."

"Let me see what you do have."

I ran to my room, got the box of photos from my desk, but then, because I didn't want to appear too eager, walked back slowly.

"They're mostly practice," I said as Melita opened the lid. "I don't know what to do with them once I take them."

Melita sifted through, going over pictures of the farm. I tried to capture the light of the ripples on the pond or the ice on the tree branches in winter, but it was hard. I had some of the animals—the goats, the sheep, one of Bear getting hosed down after having rolled in something smelly, a few of the chickens. There were also some of the sheep from last year, before and after they were slaughtered. Dad had hung the skins over the clothesline to dry and then used them for seat cushions in his car.

"These are really cool. I like how some of them are blurry. It's very arty."

"Mostly it's 'cause they don't stand still," I explained.

"Well, except for the sheepskins. It makes the photos unpredictable. People will always sit still and try to pose, but animals are more natural. They couldn't care less if they're being photographed."

"Take some of me." Melita stood up and danced around. "I won't sit still, I promise."

"I don't know," I said.

"Come on. Are you afraid?"

"No." I ran and got my camera. "It's a crappy camera," I said, as if apologizing in advance if the pictures didn't come out. "I'm saving up for a new one."

"You should get a digital camera. They're great."

"Maybe," I said. I had used one at school last year. But I didn't like it. It was too easy to change your mind and rearrange the photo. I liked to click and see what happened. The possibility for accidents is what made it exciting.

"Go ahead. I'm not posing." Melita stretched to the ceiling, then started doing jumping jacks.

I looked through the lens. I focused on her face jumping in and out of view, then her body without her face. Melita fell on the floor, yawned, and stretched in a yoga position. She had changed earlier into a bright pink tank top. The shirt stretched up to expose her bellybutton. I had a sudden desire to touch it. I clicked a couple of times and then put the camera down.

"But you are posing," I said. "You're too aware of me. Some other time." I did want to take her picture, but not yet. I wanted to get to know her better first. "I can't wait to get a new camera, but I need to make more money. I plan to get a job this summer."

"Doing what?"

"I'm not sure yet."

"You could sell your photographs," Melita suggested, sitting up at the prospect. "We could have an art show. Just think, a whole room full of your work all framed with the titles and prices on a piece of white paper taped next to them. And there could be an opening with refreshments, wine and cheese and grapes. Everyone would dress up."

I shook my head. It was a nice thought, but it was not going to happen. "First off," I said, "I don't have enough printed pieces. Second, framing is too expensive and I don't have the money. And third, my work's not good enough. Three reasons." I held up three fingers to prove my points. I didn't give the fourth reason. The fourth reason was that no one would come.

"My, my, what a pessimist you are. Maybe the first two are true, but not the last. And we can always get money. Why not ask your dad?"

"We're not rich," I said. *Unlike some*, I wanted to add. Maybe having an actress mom with lots of cash to spend made it easy. With all the clothes Melita had, it certainly seemed like she got whatever she wanted.

"I know!" Melita suddenly jumped up. "We can put on a show. A fashion show. We can ask for donations at the door and sell our ideas."

I looked at Melita's outfit. Her second one of the day.

"We just need a theme is all," she said.

"And an audience," I said.

"Well, that gives us something to think about, then, doesn't it?"

4

Days later Melita and I were sitting on the stone fence, dangling our legs and waiting for Michael to show up. Dad and Phil were fixing the barn roof, and we had already finished our chores. Melita was growing on me a little. At least I found her entertaining enough to intrigue me, and I wanted to know what made her tick. I felt like I was doing some kind of experiment. Maybe Melita would fit into my summer plans after all. She would be my study on human behavior, like a social study. I would be the next Margaret Mead, only I would study pop culture instead of Indian.

"So what do you do around here for fun?" Melita asked.

Fun? What did I do for fun? "I take pictures," I said. "I do chores."

Melita made a face. "That's not fun." Melita's own escapade with the chickens did not get off to a good start. Colorful broke his usual pattern of only going after men and came at her in a full attack. She ran screaming out of the coop. Dad wasn't about to let her off the hook, though. "You'll get it," he said. "Show that rooster you're the boss. You've got to keep going back. He's just showing off." He sounded like a cheerleader, getting her back in the game. The second time, she waved the pitchfork around her head and managed to get a few eggs. For a city girl she was pretty open to being on a farm, even if she was timid about things. And even if she still insisted on dressing up. Today she was wearing crisp white linen pants. *White? On a farm?*

"I like milking Petunia," I said. "Sometimes I read her stories." I glanced to see Melita's reaction. She looked fine.

"What kind of stories?" she asked.

"Sometimes children's books from when I was little, picture books or chapter books. I've read her *Charlotte's Web* and *Stuart Little*. Those are by E. B. White. He lived in Maine, you know. But mostly I read fairy tales."

Now Melita was looking at me like I was crazy. Her face wrinkled, but she didn't say anything, so I went on, feeling the need to justify myself. "But not the regular tales that everyone knows. I read the really gruesome ones. The ones where Cinderella's stepsisters cut off their toes and heels, and where the wolf eats Granny and doesn't just hide her in a closet."

Melita shook her head. "You're weird," she said. "You know, I've been here a week, and I've only met your brother and father, and Michael." The second meeting with Michael went much better than the first. The charm of meeting Melita must have worn off, and Michael was just as attentive to me as usual. "Don't you have any friends?" she asked.

"They live too far away to come over," I lied.

"There's no bus or anything?"

I shook my head. "You can get your driver's permit at fifteen if you take driver's ed."

"You mean I could be driving in a year?"

I nodded, hoping she'd drop the talk of friends.

"Come on, weirdo," she said, grabbing my hand and pulling me off the fence. "Let's go *dooo* something."

The day had started sunny, but now it looked to be clouding over. It was summer, but summer in Maine can be slow in coming. One day it's hot and muggy, and the next it's cold and miserable. So far this season, the bugs hadn't been too bad. But still, it was probably a far cry from the places Melita had lived in. Melita shivered and buttoned her sweater. She was dressed more appropriately for the farm than when she'd first arrived, but in her stylish sweater, fancy pants, and big-heeled sandals, it was still obvious that she was from somewhere else.

"Is there anywhere to go?" Melita asked.

"We can ride bikes to Tiny's and get ice cream. It's a couple of miles," I said.

"Sure."

"You can use Phil's bike."

We got the bikes from the barn, and with a little adjusting, Phil's fit Melita fine. We pedaled down the mile-long driveway, past the stone wall and on to where it was paved. Bear followed us to the end of the driveway, and then, like a good boy, turned back home.

"Are these your closest neighbors?" Melita asked when we passed the first house. She stopped her bike, took off her sweater, and tied it around her waist. Her T-shirt had silver sparkles on it. "Who lives there?"

"Joe and Mary Lou Silvey," I said.

"Do they have any kids?"

"They've grown up and moved away. Sometimes their grandkids visit and I baby-sit. Joe and Mary Lou were the ones who sold land to my parents," I explained. "After my parents got married, they were searching for a less complicated life. They wanted to live 'away.' They moved here to raise their children in a more natural setting. Then my mother got sick and died." I said this last part so softly, I didn't think Melita heard me.

"I'll say you're 'away' if your closest neighbors are this far. No wonder you don't see any of your friends. You must be dying to get your license."

I shrugged.

"Don't you get bored?" she asked.

"Not really. There's plenty to do."

"Yah, like work and chores."

"This is nothing. We don't even have a real working farm," I said.

"What do you mean?"

"Our farm is more of a hobby farm. Just for us. The goats are for milk, the chickens for eggs, the sheep for meat, and the garden for vegetables, but we don't sell anything, except eggs sometimes. We don't make a living off the farm. That's why Dad has another job at the seed company."

"Were your parents back-to-the-landers?" Melita asked.

I gave her a puzzled look.

"You know, people who reject modern life and technology to live off the land."

"We don't reject technology. We have a computer and a television," I said. I didn't say that Dad limited our usage of both to one hour a day. "Dad grew up not far from here. Then he went to school in New York and met my mom. They decided to come back and raise their kids here in a more natural way. That's why Joe sold him the land. He wouldn't sell to someone from away. Is that a back-to-the-lander?"

"Kind of, I guess. Our mothers were best friends. Isn't that cool?" Melita said.

I nodded. "Sure." Even though I never knew my mother and I'd never met Melita's mother, I didn't see how they could have been friends.

We started biking again and turned on to Route 11. Route 11 is the road that connects all the small towns. It ends up in Bangor. But Bangor was too far to bike to.

We continued biking without talking. As we neared Tiny's, I stood to pedal the rest of the way up the long hill. We passed the trailer park and Ken's Garage. Tiny's Market was at the top. I peeled into the parking lot. Melita was way behind. She finally caught up, panting and sweating.

"Big hill," she said, catching her breath. "And hot. I didn't think it could get hot here."

"We're inland," I explained. "On the coast it stays cooler, but we don't get much breeze here."

The clouds had settled over the hills, trapping a muggy air mass underneath. A good thunderstorm would break it. It finally felt like the first real day of summer. Tiny's had Fourth of July decorations out already.

"The reward of the hill is ice cream," I said. "And then it's all downhill on the way home."

"Thank God."

We bought a pint of Ben and Jerry's and sat outside on the picnic table.

"At least you're not so far away that you can't get good ice cream," Melita said, sucking the plastic spoon clean.

Melita ate ice cream like I did. Taking as big a spoonful as possible and then licking it off slowly. As we licked, we watched the traffic and the occasional customer pull up. I saw a flash of lightning in the distance. "We should get back before it rains."

"Already? I haven't finished catching my breath," Melita said.

I stood to get my bike, and a car drove up and parked right in front of me. I recognized a group of kids from school. Phil's friend Brian was driving.

"Hey, Phoebe." He gave a half wave.

"Hey," I said. He ran into Tiny's as the other three piled out.

I knew them all. Brian's brother, Preston. Preston's girl-friend, Lindalee, and Beth. The three of them were in my grade. Preston and Lindalee were in the popular group and never had anything to say to me, but Beth always seemed nice. We used to play together when we were in first grade, and then we stopped for no particular reason. I don't know why she hung out with Lindalee.

They usually didn't pay any attention to me, but they all did a double take at seeing me with Melita. The stripe in her hair looked especially purple in the humid haze.

"Hey there." Preston stopped in front of us. "Never seen you before."

"I'm visiting," Melita said.

"Oh, yeah?"

"Yeah."

"Where you from?" Lindalee asked in her whiny voice.

"New York City," Melita said.

They were quiet for a second as if contemplating where New York City was.

"I've been to New York," said Preston.

Lindalee punched him in the arm. "Get out," she said. "You never told me that. Why didn't you tell me that?"

"I don't tell you everything," he said, then focused on Melita. "So where in the city?"

The two of them got into a conversation about New York. Well, mostly Melita talked and Preston leered and said "Oh, yeah" a number of times.

Finally Lindalee interrupted. "Come on," she whined. "This is boring. Let's get our pizza." She dragged Preston away, leaving Beth behind.

Beth started to follow them, then turned around and said, "Hey, Phoebe, I'm going to be the art editor for the school paper next fall."

I didn't know what she expected me to say, so I said nothing.

"We're looking for entries for the first issue. I hear you take photographs. You should submit some."

"You've never seen my photographs," I said.

"Well, I bet they're good," Beth said.

Now what would make her say that? I was going to ask, when Melita interjected. "They are. I've seen them," she said. I twirled a strand of my hair and looked away.

Lindalee opened Tiny's door and yelled out in her annoying voice, "Beeethh!"

Beth waved at her, then turned back to me. "I'll call you

before the deadline," she said.

"Okay," I mumbled.

"You should definitely submit," she said again before she turned to Lindalee.

"Maybe," I said.

"See you around!" Melita called as Beth walked away.

"See you!" Beth called back.

"No wonder you don't see any of your friends," Melita said as we got on our bikes. "Either they're jerks or you don't say a word."

"They're not my friends," I mumbled. I pedaled as fast as I could, leaving Melita behind.

By the time we made it home and put the bikes away, the clouds had broken and a torrential downpour had descended on us. Melita's white pants were soaked through and had a big dirt spot from the bicycle seat.

5

"Close your eyes, Phoebe," Melita said.

I did, and the softness of the eye shadow brush flickered over my eyelid. Melita applied it so gently it reminded me of butterfly wings when you stand still and they flutter next to your cheek.

"There," she said. "Now open."

We were sitting on the big rock by the pond. Our pond was not your typical picturesque spot. It was small, shallow, and covered with lime green algae. When we were little, Phil and I were brave enough to swim in it, but now it was too slimy and I didn't like prying off the leeches. Sometimes we used the rowboat, but that wasn't terribly thrilling because you could row only to the other side and back. Skating on it in the winter was its best function.

Melita had been in Maine for two weeks already. The mornings were still chilly, but by the afternoon it was warm, even muggy. I was in a plain T-shirt and jeans. Melita wore a frilly skirt that fell just below her knees and a white T-shirt that said "happy girl" in purple cursive. She still insisted on wearing her clunky sandals, though they were showing signs of wear from walking around the farm.

Melita had her makeup kit with her. She had put some on herself first. Thick lines under her eyes. Gold, shimmery eye shadow, mascara, blush, and finally maroon lipstick on her full lips. She held up the little mirror on the powder compact to see. Then she worked on me.

Melita pointed the lipstick at me. "Now for your final touch," she said, after having done my eyes. "Go like this." She pursed her lips as though getting ready to kiss. I did the same, and she dabbed color on my lips.

"Spread it," she instructed. I mimicked her as she rubbed her upper lip over the bottom one.

"There. All done." She stood up. "You look good, Phoebe."

She handed me the mirror. I stared at my face. At first I thought I looked like a clown, with all the glitter on my eyes and deep red lips and cheeks. I stuck my tongue out at my reflection. The longer I stared, though, the cleaner and brighter I looked, especially my eyes. If I had been younger, I would have pretended that the gold was fairy dust and that I was a princess. Instead I tried to pretend that I was getting ready for a big date. For the first time ever, I had thick, dark lashes. I closed one eye to look sultry. Melita laughed. I turned to face her and pulled my T-shirt down to expose a bare shoulder. I moved forward as sexily as I could and batted my eyelashes.

"Hey, hey," I said, making my voice low. "Look at me. I'm sex-y."

Melita kept laughing, so I went on. She had a great laugh. Deep and long. I stood up and walked along the edge of the pond, trying to be a fancy woman. I rolled up my pant legs and pretended I was wearing high heels by walking on my tiptoes. The mud squished through my toes and made a sucking slurp when I picked them up. I waded into the muddy water up to my calves, then turned around, model-like. Melita clapped her hands and shouted, "Bravo!"

"Thank you, thank you. And bless you all," I said to her and my imaginary audience. I kissed the tips of my fingers and blew them into the air. "I love you all," I said and bowed again, then ran back to Melita.

She said, "You're marvelous! You're a natural."

We held hands and spun around the rock in a circle until we were dizzy, and then collapsed in the grass, out of breath but still laughing. I don't know what was so funny, but we couldn't stop.

"Let's put on a play," Melita said between laughs.

"But it has to be a funny play," I said.

"So funny that the audience will roll on the floor laughing."

"So funny that they have to clutch their tummies. Like this." I held my belly and let out a guffaw.

"So funny that they throw us all their money. Hundreds and hundreds of bills, and big bills too—tens, twenties, even hundreds! We'll be rich for the rest of our lives."

We laughed some more and were just calming down when Melita hiccupped, and that made us start all over again.

I closed my eyes and felt the earth move. We stayed there for a while, listening to our breathing and the birds singing and feeling the warmth of the sun on our faces.

"What's it like to be an actress?" I asked, still keeping my eyes closed. "I mean a real actress, like your mother?"

Melita didn't say anything, and I thought maybe she hadn't heard me. I opened my eyes. She was lying very still, her face toward the cloudless sky, in a trance.

"Melita?" I said.

She didn't move. *Shoot, I shouldn't have mentioned her mother. Now I blew it. And just when we were having fun.*

"Melita?" I said again. I saw a tear form, then fall from the corner of her eye down her temple and into her ear. She made no effort to wipe it. I reached out my hand and touched her arm near her elbow. "I'm sorry. It must be hard, huh?"

Melita kept her eyes closed, but she was really crying now. I didn't know what to do. I started to move my hand away, but she reached out with her own, grabbed mine, and placed it on her shoulder, keeping it covered with hers.

"Do you miss her?" I asked.

"I hate her." She said this with no emotion, though she was still crying.

"I see," I said, although I didn't believe she actually hated her. I say that I hate my brother plenty of times, but I don't really mean it. I was curious about Melita's mother. I knew what my dad had told me about her, but I wanted to know more. Maybe it would help me know my own mother. I had been afraid to bring it up before.

"What happened?" There. I had asked it. The question was big and fat. Melita opened her eyes and stared straight up.

She let go of my hand and wiped her face. The mascara smudged across her cheek, leaving black streaks. She barely made a sound, just took quick, delicate breaths. She needed to blow her nose, and I wished I had a tissue to offer her.

"You wanna know? You really want to know?"

I nodded.

"She's crazy. That's what." Melita studied my expression. I tried to make none. She went on. "She's always been crazy. She says it's part of the actor's lifestyle, but I don't think so. I think it's just her."

"How is she" —I paused a second— "crazy?"

"She sings all the time, even in public, really loud. She talks to anyone who will listen, strangers in the grocery store, homeless people on the street. And those are some of the okay things."

We both sat for a minute looking out over the green pond. Gerelyn sounded like fun. Sometimes I wished my father was more fun, loose like that. I wondered if my mother had been the more relaxed one.

"Sometimes, when it's bad," Melita continued, "I get up in the morning and she's just sitting on the couch, crying for no reason. And she's still there when I get home from school. We're always moving 'cause she gets tired of being in one place. 'We need a fresh start,' she says. Or 'change is the only constant.' She's always saying she's a bad mother, that she could do better for me. But she's not, she's doing her best, I know she is."

I stayed quiet, too afraid to say anything.

"And then, one day I came home and she was on the couch, just lying there. Not moving. She didn't see me. I thought she was dead. I had to call 911."

"But she's getting help now, isn't she?" I asked.

Melita grunted. "Yah, I guess. That's what she says."

"How—" The word got out before I could stop it.

Melita looked straight at me and said, "It's okay, Phoebe. It's what everyone wants to know. She took a bottle of sleeping pills. She passed out. Funny thing, I should've known. She was acting weird all morning. Said she had some stuff to do by herself. I should've known."

I put my hand back on Melita's shoulder. "I'm sorry." My voice came out in a cracked whisper. I couldn't imagine what it must have been like for Melita to come home and see her mom like that.

Melita put her hand over mine again.

I wanted to say something more. "Does she drink?" I asked. The second I saw Melita's face I knew it was the wrong question. I wanted to kick myself.

"Not everyone who's crazy is an alcoholic, you know." She shook my arm away and shot me a look. "You are so provincial, Phoebe. Don't you know anything?" She stood up and brushed some twigs off her skirt. "I don't want to talk to you anymore," she said. "Don't follow me." She turned and walked toward the meadow.

I sat on the rock for a while. *Stupid, stupid, stupid me.* I'd blown it. I stared at my reflection in the murky water. I tried splashing the makeup off with some water but scooped up gobs of algae instead. I couldn't even clean my face right.

Later that night, Melita came into my room.

"If I'm going to be here all summer, then we're going to have to like each other," she said.

"Okay," I said, putting my book down.

40

"You can't help it if you don't know certain things. Look where you've been living."

"Okay," I said again, not sure whether to feel insulted or not.

"Truth is, Phoebe, you're the first person I've said any of that stuff to. Since . . . since it happened."

"I won't ask anymore."

"No, it's okay, Phoebe. It's probably good for me to talk about it. That's what Mom would say. As crazy as she is, she does have some good advice sometimes. It was her idea that I come here. So are we friends?"

I guess we were friends. As much as we could be. As different as we were.

I nodded. And then, to my surprise, Melita leaned over and kissed me on the cheek. A soft peck that lingered for a second, her lips pressed onto my skin, making a warm spot.

"Good night," she said and ran off to her room before I could say anything. I rubbed my fingers where she'd kissed, thinking how nice it was to feel her close to me.

Just when I thought Melita hated me and hated everything about this place, she turned and completely surprised me. She was unlike anyone I'd ever known.

6

So I've been thinking about this fashion show," Melita announced. We sat outside eating breakfast, yogurt and granola with sliced peaches. I had just finished milking Petunia.

Phil came out with two dozen eggs. "Feeling lazy, girls?" he asked.

"We're figuring something out," Melita said.

"Oh, like what?"

"You wouldn't be interested," I said quickly. The last thing I wanted was to have Phil make fun of me.

"It's girl stuff," Melita said.

"Well, excuse me for living then." He brushed by us with the keys to the truck. "I'm going over to Crystal's today anyway. Her mom wants to buy some eggs." Since Melita had arrived, Phil had been spending more and more time at Crystal's, which was fine with me. He waved to us as he backed out, the wheels scattering gravel on the grass.

"So what about the show?" I asked Melita.

"We could dress up in really funky outfits. I love designing outfits."

She stood up and turned around, demonstrating that day's creation: a white blouse with poofy capped sleeves and a scoop neck, tucked into red-and-black-checked shorts with a wide black belt and platform flip-flops.

"I don't know." I frowned. "That's too girlie for me."

"You're a girl, for crying out loud! What's so wrong with that?"

I shrugged.

Melita took me by the shoulders. "Celebrate your womanhood! Accept your feminine side. Be free!" She stood up and spun around. "It's great being a girl, haven't you heard? What do you think our mothers and their mothers and their mothers before them and back and back all the way to women's suffrage worked for?"

I shrugged again. "Equality?" I said.

Melita shook her head. "For us. For us to enjoy being who we are." She collapsed on the grass. "Besides, who's girlie? You're the one who reads all these romantic fairy tales to your goat."

"That's not fair," I protested. "Those are tales, not real life. Fantasy."

"And that makes it okay? Women can be oppressed in fantasy? What do you think leads to real life? Fairy tale girls who are waiting to be rescued by a prince make real girls long for the same thing. They're role models, whether we like it or not. Besides, I've seen the way you look at Michael."

That hurt, but I wasn't about to admit it. "There are plenty of strong female characters in fairy tales," I said.

"Yeah, who?"

I thought for a minute. "Well, there's Gretel. She's the one who pushes the witch into the oven."

"Yeah, but it took her long enough."

43

"And there's Snow White, who sends the huntsman back with an animal heart instead of her own."

"She was just saving her own butt. Besides, she runs away and hides with dwarfs. Any others?"

"The princess in *Bluebeard,* who tricks the king and escapes." I neglected to add "with the help of her three brothers."

"Okay, so there's three. Out of how many fairy tales?"

"Some of the other versions have stronger characters," I said. But it was true, the ones I had read mostly didn't.

"Well, don't you think it's interesting and kind of sad that the best-known fairy tales have the weakest women? They're all saved in the end by some man, or by a magic spell, or both. I think it's time to liberate the fairy tale women." Melita raised her fist like she was ready to fight a campaign.

I actually agreed with her. But I wasn't ready to admit it, and I was enjoying watching her get all riled up. So I let her go on for a bit.

"We need modern fairy tale role models. Ones that girls can be proud of and identify with. Ones who accept their femininity but aren't afraid to fight."

"Or get dirty," I added, giving Melita a sidelong glance.

"Or get dirty," she repeated. "Powerful, strong female heroines who do not need or even want to be rescued by a man. Ones who wear 'girl power' T-shirts and combat boots instead of glass slippers they can't run in, but who can still look sexy and show some cleavage."

"If they have any," I said, glancing down.

Melita laughed. "Right."

"They could still put sparkles in their hair, though," I said.

And suddenly the idea hit us. As if a light bulb had gone on in our heads at the same time.

"That's it," Melita said.

"The show," I said.

"Fairy tales," we both said.

We decided we would pick six fairy tale women. First we had a debate over whether to refer to them as women or girls. Most of them were portrayed as young, but by today's standards they seemed older, so the modern fairy tale girl would be more like a woman. Except for Gretel and Little Red Riding Hood, who were still young enough to be girls. And those two don't meet men.

We also decided to pick the well-known characters. It wouldn't make sense to pick ones that were so obscure no one knew their stories. I wanted to use the princess from *Bluebeard* (one of my favorite stories), but she didn't even have a name.

We would reidentify them as modern young women, sexy and feminine, still a bit old-fashioned and proper in their manners, but with more power. They would be aware of their strength and know how to use it, almost like their evil counterparts the witch or the stepmother. But these women would use their power for good and not resort to magic unless absolutely necessary. Magic seems like the cop-out solution if you ask me. Too easy.

And somehow all this would come across in their attitudes and the outfits Melita and I would create. I wasn't sure how all this was going to play out, but so far, I was willing to go along with it. I knew, though, that I did not want to be one of the ones onstage, dressed up. I'd be happy to come up with ideas, but parading across the stage in front of people was another story. Not that I thought anyone in this town would come, but I wasn't going to tell that to Melita. The pleasure would be in the planning. And now that we had the idea to modernize fairy tale women, I was much more excited.

The six characters we agreed on were Little Red Riding Hood, Cinderella, Rapunzel, Sleeping Beauty, Snow White, and the Little Mermaid. The Little Mermaid wasn't technically a Grimm story, but we figured she was well known enough to count.

"The problem is," Melita said, "where are we going to find material and clothes around here?"

"What about your suitcase?" I said, half joking.

"Well, I might have some things we can use. I don't suppose you have any retro stores or anything around here?"

"I don't think so. Maybe in Bangor. I know there's a Goodwill." I didn't add that Dad got most of our clothes from there. "But I have something even better," I said. "Follow me." I led Melita into the house and up the attic stairs. There were piles of boxes in the attic marked with labels like "Phoebe and Phil/Early Art" and "Baby Clothes." My dad couldn't get rid of a thing. I moved the boxes, looking for one in particular.

"What are you looking for?" Melita asked.

"It's here somewhere. Dad saved everything." I handed Melita a box. And there it was in the corner. An oversize wooden trunk with heavy black handles and a faded white label that read "Carol/Clothes." Together we lugged it to the middle of the room.

"This is my mother's stuff from school," I explained. "She collected material and costumes to use for set designs and plays. She wanted to be a costume designer." I lifted the lid.

"This is so great!" Melita said, pulling out a bag of cloth ribbons in a rainbow of colors and patterns. "Wow, no wonder our moms were friends. They were both in the theater." She put on a purple felt hat, pulled the brim over her eyes, and tied one of the ribbons around her neck in a bow. It made a shimmering white choker. Then she unfolded a square of gold burlap. "We've probably got everything we need in here. It's as if your mom knew it would be used someday."

"Or my dad, since he saved it all," I said. "I don't think my mother ever got to use it after she moved here. I mean, where in Plattville would you wear this stuff?"

"Well, it was meant for us, then."

The last time I had seen the trunk was when I was about six or seven. Dad was moving some things to the attic, and I was helping. I had opened the trunk and started poring over the beautiful fabrics. He came running over and stopped me. "Maybe when you're older. This stuff is too delicate," he'd said. But I was older now, and the trunk was perfect. Plus I was actually able to provide something cool for once. Melita pranced around in her hat and ribbons and smiled at me.

I found the dog costume my mom had made for Phil. It was a Velcro outfit complete with a tail and a dog-shaped hood. It was a fake-fur material in mottled brown, just like Bear. I held it up to me. It was small, but the hood part fit on my head like a beret. I draped the rest of it over my shoulder and petted it like it was a ferret or something.

"Who am I?" I asked Melita.

"The baby bear in *Goldilocks*?"

"No," I said, digging through the trunk for something red. I found a pair of red pleather pants and pulled them up over my shorts.

"I'm Little Red Riding Hood. And this is the wolf I slaughtered." I paraded around the attic with my fresh kill.

"Ohhh, that's good," Melita said. She held up a silvery dress. "This looks like the Snow Queen. Maybe we should do her."

We started making piles of things that we could use. Ribbons, material, long flowy dresses, a little white Pilgrim bonnet, and stuff from the 1960s and '70s— psychedelic shirts, hippie skirts, and minidresses.

Melita pulled out a green turtle outfit. So tiny, it was hard to believe I once fit into it. "This is adorable."

"That was my Halloween costume when I was two," I said.

"You must have looked so cute. Can you imagine?"

I looked at the little shell of soft fabric. A two-year-old could have pulled it over her neck to almost make her head disappear like a real turtle. I tried to remember wearing it or my mom making it. Measuring me to get it to fit. Trying it on me. I couldn't remember anything except vague stories Phil had told.

"Some of this stuff is even wearable." Melita tried on a

yellow blouse with extra-large orange and pink daisies all over it. It did look like something she'd wear. She pushed her chest out. "Look, a daisy on each tit."

I stared at her round breasts, started to flush, and turned away.

"Your mom must have been very cool," she said. "Don't you wish you knew her?"

I nodded, unable to say anything. I unzipped the red pants and took them off. I wondered if my mom had worn these clothes or just collected them. Was she bold and daring? How did she go over in Plattville? She wasn't from here, like Dad. Did she even want to be here?

"Those pants looked good on you," Melita said.

"They were too hot." I folded them and placed them in the pile.

"We'll definitely have to use them for Little Red Riding Hood." She came over and lifted one of my braids. Her fingers brushed ever so slightly on my shoulder and sent a little shiver through me. Her breath was warm on my neck as she inspected my hair. She pulled one braid out to its full length and then tugged gently at the base of it, almost like she was massaging my hair. Her fingers moved nimbly up and down my braid, back and forth. I couldn't remember the last time anyone had touched my hair like that. Suddenly I wanted to reach over and pull Melita even closer, to caress her creamy brown skin and feel her lips. I wanted to bury my nose in her scrunchy hair and take a good whiff of her shampoo.

"You will definitely have to play Rapunzel," she said. I didn't have the heart to protest. She coiled both braids on top of my head. "In fact, if we cut these off, we could make one extra-long one. Have you ever thought of getting your hair cut?"

I opened my eyes, and something in me went weak. "Yah," I said. "I've thought about it."

7

One night after dinner was over and the sun was starting to set, I had the sudden urge to show Melita something I hadn't shown many people.

"Where are we going?" she asked when I dragged her out of the house.

"You'll see." I led her through the tall grasses to the other side of the pond where the weeping willow stood.

"This tree was planted the day after I was born," I told her. "My dad planted it in honor of my birth." I pointed to a stone grave marker underneath the tree with the name Carol Olsen Sharp carved into it. "And this is where my mother's ashes were buried two years later. I think of this tree as both of ours."

The lowest branch of the willow bent over the pond in a U shape. I walked across it and sat down with my legs over the water. Melita followed, her arms stretched out like a tightrope walker's. She started to lose her balance.

"Grab hold of the branch above you," I said.

She tried but lost her footing and almost slipped. She sat down instead and shimmied the rest of the way over.

"This takes skill," she said when she reached me. She leaned against my shoulder. The wind whispered through the willow leaves as the sky turned pink from the setting sun.

"It's pretty," she said.

"I come here to think sometimes," I said.

"Do you miss your mother?" she asked.

"I never knew her. I was too young to remember."

"But don't you miss having a mother?"

"Sometimes." I shrugged. "Do you miss having a father?"

Now Melita shrugged. "Not really. I don't know what it would be like to have him around."

"I know what you mean."

We sat for a few minutes watching the algae swirl about in the murky water below. I was conscious of Melita's body close to mine, her breath going in and out.

"Let's go," I said, suddenly nervous.

We balanced our way off the branch and went inside and upstairs. I expected Melita to go to her room, but she followed me to the aquarium on my bookshelf where I kept my pet turtle, Fred. I picked Fred up and sat down on the floor with him in my lap.

"Have you ever kissed a boy?" Melita asked randomly. Fred poked his head out and started to slowly crawl across my lap. I watched him with my head down, sort of pretending I hadn't heard her question but also thinking of how to answer it.

"You haven't, have you?" she asked.

I laughed nervously. "Well, kind of," I said.

"What is 'kind of' kissing? Either you kiss or you don't."

I explained to her how Michael had kissed me a few

months ago on my birthday. "You're thirteen now, almost a woman," he'd said, and leaned over and touched his lips to my cheek, just to the side of my lips. If I'd turned the right way, it would have been on the lips.

"That's not a real kiss. That's more like a brother-sister kiss."

"Eww," I said. I didn't think it was that at all.

"I've kissed four boys," Melita said. "Real kissing."

My stomach did a small flip. Jealousy?

"Want me to show you how?" she asked. Melita picked Fred up with two fingers and put him back in his cage. He climbed into his puddle of water and hid, with only his tiny eyes and nose bulging out.

"Like a fairy tale. I'll be the boy, the prince. You can be the princess," she said.

"I don't know," I said.

"We're pretending, Phoebe. You want to know how to do it when you're with a boy, right? When your prince charming finally comes along, you want to be ready."

"I guess." Maybe if I had known how to kiss on my birthday, the kiss with Michael would have been different.

"Now," Melita went on, "you're the girl."

"Duh," I said.

Melita ignored me. "The girl has to make the boy feel that it's okay to make a move. Give me a sign."

I winked, batted my eyelashes, and made some kissing sounds.

"Not like that, goofball. More subtle. You move close like this." She leaned into me.

"All right," I said as our shoulders touched. "What now?"

"Just follow me."

We were sitting cross-legged on the floor. Fred was still watching us, bug-eyed. Melita shifted closer so that our knees touched. She leaned into me. I leaned into her. She put her hands on my shoulders. I put my hands on her shoulders. She brushed the hair from my forehead. I brushed her fading purple streak.

"Okay, okay. You don't have to do everything I do." She sat back.

"But you said—"

"I know. I know. Forget that. Try to be more natural. Do what feels right. Relax."

"How can I relax when I know we're going to kiss? This is too weird."

"Come here." Melita turned me around and started massaging my shoulders. "You're so tight. Just relax."

I bent my head down and let her massage my neck. We were quiet. I could feel her breath. And then somehow my face was facing hers, and she was coming closer and closer. I thought of those old black-and-white movies where the kissing scene is in slow motion. Melita's eyes were closed, and her cheeks had a pink glow as if the sunset from the window behind her was shining through.

She opened one eye. "You have to close your eyes," she whispered.

I squinted my eyes so they looked closed but I could still peek.

She spoke in a low voice. "Oh, Phoebe. You're so pretty. So pretty I could kiss you."

Her lips touched mine. I tried to imagine the fireworks that go off in the old movies at this point. But they didn't.

Maybe because this is just practice, I thought. I thought of Sleeping Beauty. The kiss that brings the princess back to life. Was Melita going to bring me back to life? I thought of Beauty and the Beast and the Frog Prince. The kiss that transforms the prince back into his true form. Was I going to transform Melita back to her true form?

Melita's lips were soft and moist. I wondered if a boy's lips would feel the same. I tried to remember Michael's on my cheek. But I could only remember the kiss on the cheek that Melita had given me the other night.

She stopped, pulled her lips away for a second, and said in a breathy whisper, "Kiss back."

I kissed back. It felt nice. For a moment we stayed like that, with our lips together. And then gently, Melita nibbled on my lower lip. I laughed a little but kept kissing.

I'm kissing, I thought. *I'm kissing Melita.* And it was exciting.

She opened her mouth slightly. Placed her hand on my chin.

"Ach!" I said and pushed her away. It wasn't mean, it just surprised me.

We looked at each other, not saying anything. Our faces were still close.

"That was nice, Phoebe," she said.

"Yah," I breathed.

"But enough for now. I'll see you in the morning."

"Yah," I said.

Melita touched my hair. Then she got up and called out good night as she shut the door. I listened to the sound of her footsteps as she walked down the hall.

I tapped on Fred's tank. "Hey, Fred," I said. He was

hiding completely in his shell. I touched his back, but he stayed in there.

I lay down on the bed, looking at the cracks in the ceiling. I had long ago figured out an image for every crack. When I was four I discovered one that looked like a lowercase *e*. Later on, other images emerged. There was an airplane with a bird riding on top and a crown with three points and an elf wearing a floppy hat. But now, the cracks seemed to take on completely new shapes, all resembling various parts of the human body from pictures I'd seen in biology books.

I thought of Preston, the cutest boy in class. All the girls had a crush on Preston. I thought of Phil's friend Brian, who, along with Phil, used to wrestle me to the floor and tickle me until I yelled for Dad. I thought of how I wanted to marry Michael someday. I thought of all the fairy tales I'd read. How the girl gets the boy. What if I loved a girl?

I could still feel Melita's touch. Her hands on my back. Her lips on mine. How she tasted like strawberries and smelled of honey.

I put my hand on my belly. My skin was soft and a little mushy.

I grabbed my pillow and hugged it. I started to cry. Then I thought of Melita's kiss, how she said it was just practice, but that only made me cry more. I cried long and hard like I hadn't cried since I was a baby, though in a weird way it felt really good to just bawl that way. And eventually I fell asleep exhausted and worn out from all my tears.

a couple of folding chairs, and some candles. We'd hide out and tell ghost stories on rainy days. But since high school, Phil hardly went up anymore. Except, one day just before school got out, I went up to read. I heard some rustling in the dark and yelled, thinking it might be a rat. Phil and Crystal emerged from under the blankets, their clothes and hair all rumpled. Crystal's shirt was unbuttoned. I knew they'd been fooling around, but they both pretended nothing had happened. I wondered how far they would have gone if I hadn't interrupted. I wonder how far they've gone since.

"What a cool place," Melita said, looking around at all the old stuff.

I opened one of the folding chairs in front of the window, dusted it off, and sat down. "Do magic," I said. I handed her the scissors.

I felt the motion as they moved through the air.

"Whirrrr, whirrrr," Melita said, pretending the scissors were an airplane landing on my head. She lifted one of my long braids.

"Whirrrr," she repeated. Then she cut. It sounded as though she were slicing through steel wool. Slice, slice, slice. And suddenly the braid fell off in her hand. Just like that. She waved it over my head like a lasso before dropping it in my lap.

It fell across my folded hands like a coiled snake. Then, slice, slice, slice again, and plop as the second braid landed next to the first. Two lifeless objects in my lap. Melita went on snipping.

"This is gonna be great, Phoeb. You're gonna love it. I think maybe I've found my calling. I'm destined to be a new wave stylist."

Melita went on, but I tuned her out. What had I done? Everyone always commented on my hair. It was the only thing they ever commented on. What a pretty color, how cute I was with braids and freckles, a real farm girl. I hated my braids and loved them at the same time.

"Long hair is so out!" Melita said when she first suggested the haircut. "Your hair is so unruly. It'll look hot short. Short and sexy. I won't do anything severe, I promise."

I wanted to look sexy. As Melita snipped and shaped, I wondered if I did. When she did the front, she leaned down and peered in my eyes.

"You have such dark green eyes," she said. "Like olives."

I felt my face go red as I fingered the braids in my lap.

"And you're pretty when you blush," she said.

Her lips were close enough to touch. I thought about kissing them. I wanted to. My heart was racing. I was going to, when all of a sudden Melita stepped back and announced that she was done.

I came out of my trance. What were these feelings? I quickly hid them away. No feelings. Just short hair.

"The hardest part was getting through those braids," she said. "The rest was easy."

"How does it look?" I asked.

Melita raised her fist in the air and said with a British accent, "Fab-u-lous!"

There was no mirror in the loft, but I lifted my hand to my head and let out an "Oh."

I tugged my hair down to my ears. Not as short as

Melita's, but still a shock. I shook my head and couldn't help laughing as the hair fluttered back into place.

"Wow," I said.

"Now who's going to want to rumple your hair?"

I was about to say "You are," when the boards in the other room creaked. "Shhhh." I put my finger over my lips and mouthed to Melita, "Someone's here."

The boards creaked again. What if it was Dad? What if he saw what I had done? He loved my hair. "So like your mother's," he would tell me over and over again. How was I going to hide it from him forever?

"Hey! Phoebe! You up here?" Phil. I breathed. But still I didn't want him to see me. I grabbed a blanket, threw it over my head, and sat back down just as he came up.

"There you are," he said. "What're you two up to?"

It was pretty obvious, I guess, with Melita standing behind me holding a pair of scissors, strands of red hair at her feet, and the end of a braid sticking out from the blanket.

"Nothing," I mumbled.

"Phil," Melita said. "You are just in time to see my masterpiece. Presenting"—she paused for effect, then pulled the blanket off me—"the New Phoebe! Ta-da!"

I looked up. Phil stared. No one said anything.

Finally Melita broke the silence. "Well?"

Phil shook his head and started to laugh. "Oh, God, Phoebe! Dad's going to kill you." He laughed and laughed. "You look like a plucked chicken."

"Shut up!" I shouted. It couldn't be that bad. What did he know, anyway?

"What on earth made you cut your hair?" he asked.

61

"For your information, long hair is out!" I said.

"Boy, oh, boy." He kept shaking his head. "Dad's gonna kill you."

"I still have the braids." I held them up. They were beginning to unravel.

He slapped his knee and laughed even harder. "Maybe we can sew 'em back on and no one will notice."

"You just don't know what style is, Phil," Melita protested. "Phoebe needs to get with the times. She's not going to live on this farm all her life."

I wasn't so sure about that. Suddenly I didn't want to go anywhere, not the way Phil kept staring and laughing. Maybe I'd live in the hayloft for the rest of my life. At least until my hair grew back.

"I almost forgot why I came up here," Phil said all of a sudden. "Dad says Petunia is about to drop the kid, and we have to help, or at least watch, and be educated on the wonderful birthing process of mammals."

Melita dropped the scissors. "Oh my God! Really? Come on, Phoeb. She's gonna have 'em. She's gonna have the babies."

The three of us scurried across the boards and one by one climbed down the ladder. Phil, Melita, then me bringing up the rear. I shoved my braids in my back pocket. They swung down my butt and hit the back of my legs like thick ropes.

When we got to Petunia's stall, she was lying down and Dad was kneeling next to her. Already, a head was appearing. Dad stood ready to pull if Petunia needed it. Petunia was heaving and sighing. She looked extremely uncomfortable.

"Stand back and give her room," Dad said. "So far she's doing all right. Michael's inside warming milk and getting the bottles ready."

"Don't they drink milk from their mother?" Melita whispered.

"No," I said. "That would make Petunia dry."

"Oh," she whispered back with a blank stare.

"We drink the milk, too," I explained, "and if we let the kid drink it all, there wouldn't be enough. So we milk her first and then let the kid drink it from baby bottles."

Melita crinkled her nose. I wondered if she was thinking of the time I gave her some goats' milk. She coughed and spit it in the sink. I guess goats' milk tastes funny if you're not used to it. I still hate drinking cows' milk from the store because it tastes like cardboard, not smooth and creamy like Petunia's.

"Look, look, here it comes." Dad gets so excited, like a kindergartner, over things like this. The baby's head was out, wet and slick and a little bloody. Petunia heaved and raised her head, a worried look in her eyes.

"It's okay, Petunia. Dad's helping," I comforted.

Dad grabbed hold of the head and pulled the rest of the body out. It lay in a small pile by Petunia's belly, a mass of long, spindly legs covered in a bloody ooze. The afterbirth came next.

Melita covered her eyes but peeked between her fingers. She made a few groaning noises. Even I thought the afterbirth was disgusting. A smelly and slimy blob of raspberry Jell-O.

"There's another!" Dad shouted as a second head appeared.

Petunia was already licking the first one clean, and it was beginning to look like a baby goat. It was light brown with a darker shade of brown on its tail and down its front legs.

"Is it a boy or a girl?" I asked.

"This first one's a girl," Dad said.

And then the second one dropped out.

"Another girl," Dad shouted. "Wahoo!"

I looked to see if Melita was still watching. She was. We moved closer so that our elbows touched.

Petunia was breathing fast and heavy.

"What's wrong with her?" Melita asked.

"Giving birth is difficult," Dad said and for the first time turned around to look at us. He stared at me for a second and gave me a quizzical look. I wasn't sure why until he said, "Your hair."

I felt my head. My hair had not miraculously grown back. It was still short.

"Here they are," I said and pulled out the braids from my pocket.

"Dad!" Phil pointed to Petunia, who was panting even harder. There was a third kid coming out.

"Triplets!" Dad turned back to Petunia. I breathed again, the pressure off me for a second. But the way Petunia was heaving and whining didn't sound normal.

"It's upside down," Dad said. "She can't get it out."

"Should we call the vet?" Phil asked, all set to run for help.

"Not yet." Dad reached his hand into Petunia and tried to ease the legs out.

Petunia kept panting and pushing, and Dad kept

pulling. Finally a leg appeared. A second leg and then a third poked out with Dad pulling gently on the other end. "I think I can manage," he said. "I think it'll come."

Melita reached to grab my hand, but I was wringing my braids tightly with both hands. I let them drop and took her hand and squeezed it.

It seemed like hours, but Petunia and Dad finally managed. This one was smaller than the other two, but like them she was a girl and she was alive.

We let Petunia lick them clean for a while, then Dad gathered the first one in his arms.

"Let's bring 'em inside," he said.

Phil picked up the second one. She, like the first, was light brown but with black markings. I picked up the last one. She was small but had those long, gawky goat legs. Her fur was the color of cream, and there was the thinnest dark brown stripe going down her back from her head to the tip of her tail. She was beautiful. Melita walked with me, her hand holding on to my elbow.

"This is so exciting," she said. "Wait until my mom hears about this. This is the most *amazing* thing I have *ever* seen."

We marched into the kitchen like a parade. This was the only time that farm animals were allowed in the house. Michael was standing over the sink with the bottles.

"Look at that!" he exclaimed when he saw all three.

"All girls, too," I told him.

"Look at you!" he shouted in surprise and touched his head. Once again I had forgotten my hair. Was everyone going to do this when they saw me? I hadn't even seen it for myself yet.

65

"Melita cut my hair," I said as the kid bleated in my arms.

Dad gave me a hard, cold stare. "I guess so," he said.

Phil whispered, "I told ya. He's gonna kill you."

"Well, it looks good," Michael said, trying to break the tension.

"We will deal with this later." Dad sighed. "Right now we've got triplets, and they're probably starving."

After we fed the kids, letting them suck the warm milk from the bottles, we put them in the barn in a stall of their own. They were already walking, fumbling on wobbly legs. While everyone was watching them, I slipped over to Petunia's stall at the other end. She was still lying down but looked okay. I stroked her between the ears and listened to her breathe in and out.

"You had three beautiful little girls," I whispered. "You did a great job, doing all that. You'll see them soon." And then I noticed my two braids wound in a coil next to her. They had some blood and hay on them, but I picked them up anyway. With a little cleaning they would still make a perfect Rapunzel costume.

I went back to the house and upstairs to my room. I wound my braids up and placed them in my top dresser drawer, next to where I'd put Lambchops's tail. Then, I finally checked out my new look for myself.

9

The haircut wasn't bad. Not bad at all. Melita knew how to cut. It took a few days to get used to washing and brushing it, and it was weird to feel so much of my neck. But it was much easier to deal with. Just wash, shake, and go. Even Dad had to admit it was easier. He'd hated dealing with my hair as much as I did, which is why he gave it up years ago. But I knew he was sad. "I'm my own person," I explained to him. He looked at me wistfully and said, "I know, sweetheart, I know." But he said he still had to punish me for not asking for permission and for doing it behind his back.

My punishment was no trip to town on Saturday. Which meant no library. Every few weeks I go into town with Dad to check out a batch of new books. Since I hadn't finished my last batch, this wasn't so bad, but I still would've liked to have gone with Melita.

Melita's punishment was that she *did* have to go to town with Dad and hang out at the library. Dad liked to try to make his punishments good for us in some educational way.

That morning Melita came into my room dressed for town in a black-and-white-striped halter top and matching capri pants with a silver choker around her neck and her criss-cross sandals. Her tattoo was freshly redrawn.

"This will be the first day we'll be apart since I got here," she said.

That seemed hard to believe. Melita had been there a month. It was mid-July already. The Fourth had come and gone with little fanfare. We went to a town picnic, and I did my best to avoid seeing anyone. Melita chatted with Beth, and I, as usual, said little.

I looked at my reflection in the mirror and played with my hair. I could twirl the curls against themselves so that they straightened, and then when I let go they bounced back to a tight q shape.

"It'll be really cute with some little barrettes in it. Here." She took out the pink barrettes from her own hair and started fussing with mine.

We watched each other in the mirror. Every time I was with Melita now I couldn't help smiling. Even Dad had noticed it. "Having a friend must be good for you, Phoebe. I haven't seen you this happy in a long time."

But it was more than that. When I was with Melita I never knew what would happen. Ever since I could remember, my life had been so easy and predictable. School, chores, reading, the animals, my family; even my photographs seemed dull and predictable. I hadn't read as much or taken as many pictures this summer, and yet I did feel happy.

When Melita finished with the barrettes, she ran her hand up the back of my neck. It gave me chills.

"Are you cold?" she asked.

"No. That feels nice."

She massaged my neck. I closed my eyes, then opened them. The maple tree outside my window was bursting in full summer green. It couldn't get much fuller or greener.

"See that tree?" I pointed. "That's how I feel."

Melita laughed. "You come up with the funniest things."

It wasn't supposed to be funny, but it had made Melita laugh, which made me all happy inside.

Our faces were so close I could feel her breath, see her pores. I wanted to press my mouth against hers. I wanted to taste her lips again. Neither of us said a thing, and the space between us narrowed even more.

"Melita? Are you up there?" Dad's voice from below. Melita and I broke apart just as he appeared in the doorway. "Phoebe, Melita," he said.

Melita and I stood side by side, military straight. Her face was as red as mine felt. I tried not to look guilty. Why should I feel guilty, anyway? We hadn't done anything.

Dad stood there looking from one of us to the other. Finally he said, "Phoebe, I want you to reflect on what you've done. It may have worked out okay, but you need to ask for my permission before you go making radical changes. Understand?"

For a second I forgot he was talking about my hair. I almost sighed with relief when I realized he was. I nodded.

"This is your punishment, don't forget."

"I won't forget," I said.

"Good. Melita, I'll meet you downstairs." He turned to go, then turned back and said, "Before I forget, Melita, your mother called and wants you to call her tonight."

Melita and I exchanged looks. Her mom had only called a few times. Melita's cell phone didn't work on the farm, so she had to resort to using a regular land phone. Melita said her mother didn't even use regular phones anymore, unless she had to. All she had was her cell.

"She sounded good," Dad said before going downstairs.

"I'm sorry you can't come into town," Melita said, avoiding mentioning her mom. "It'll be boring without you."

"Town is pretty boring anyway," I said. "It's not like New York must be."

"I can't believe I have to spend three hours in the library all by myself."

"I can't believe I can't spend three hours in the library with you," I said.

"Do you want me to get you anything?"

"Nah," I said. I handed her a book from my desk. "You can renew this, though. I haven't gotten to it yet."

She read the title. "*Jane Eyre*. I've heard of that. Any good?"

"So far it is," I said. "It's about an orphan who's very plain. But I'm pretty sure it turns into a love story. I'll let you know when I finish it."

"You know, we're kind of like orphans," she said.

"Huh?" Secretly I identified with Jane Eyre, though not for that reason. It was more for the fact that she was plain and lonely and misunderstood.

"I mean, you're motherless and I'm pretty much father-less, so if we were one person we'd be an orphan."

The car horn honked outside. "My dad's enough parent for everyone," I said. "You'd better go."

She ran down the stairs, but then just as quickly ran back up.

"I forgot to give you something," she said.

"What?"

"This." She bent her head and kissed me on the lips. A nice, soft kiss. Then she left once more. A smile spread across my face, and I felt my cheeks turn as red as a maple leaf in autumn. I wanted to jump and scream with delight.

I waited until I heard the car pull out of the driveway. I felt good, but I couldn't help but wonder if Dad had guessed what we were doing, and if so, what would he think? Weren't we a little too old to be "practicing" like this? None of the girls at school needed to practice kissing, as far as I knew. And deep down, or maybe even not so deep, I knew it wasn't practicing. Suddenly, my mood changed, like a shift in the wind, from elation to my old stupid self.

I looked in the mirror once again. I stuck out my tongue. "You are ugly," I said out loud. I heard Melita's words telling me how pretty I was, but my own words blocked them out. "U-G-L-Y. Ugly."

"What're you looking at?" I sneered at Fred, who'd come out of his shell. I wrinkled my nose and twisted my lips to make a really ugly face. He retreated and curled up in his little home, too scared, or maybe too smart, to stay out.

Suddenly I had to move. I ran downstairs, through the front door, into the barn, and straight to the goats' stall. All three kids were curled up together, sleeping. I crawled in with them. I lay down on the hay and burrowed my head into the smallest one, the cream-colored one. She woke and tried to scurry away. I held on to her, more forcefully than I had intended. The other two woke up. I tried to gather all three in a circle to hug them, but they managed to run away and huddle in the far corner. They still had difficulty walking on their spindly legs, especially the little one. She reminded me of long, curly pasta.

"I'm going to call you Noodles," I said to her, even though we had already named her Rosebud, and the other two Jasmine and Tulip. Dad said flower names made female goats produce sweet milk.

They looked at me with their big dark eyes. "I'm your friend," I said and moved slowly so as not to frighten them, but when I was almost close enough to touch them they darted to the other side. I tried again, but even on their new legs they were quick.

I chased them around the stall. This time I managed to grab hold of Noodles and scoop her up around her legs. She straightened her long neck to my face, sniffed my hair, and then nibbled on my ear.

"There, see?" I told her. "I'm not so bad." I burrowed my nose in her soft hair. "You'll be my friend, won't you?" Still holding her in my arms so she couldn't run away, I lay down, with Noodles in the curve of my body. I stroked her head and, in a soothing voice, said, "There, there. It's okay. You'll be fine. Don't worry." Eventually she did get comfortable, or gave up trying to escape at any rate, because she nestled against me.

The other two, realizing that I was harmless, came over and nuzzled their cold, wet noses under my chin. I closed my eyes.

"I wish you were my sisters," I said. I knew, though,

that I couldn't hide with them forever. All my life I wanted a best friend, someone I could share everything with. I never thought I would find one. And now that I had, I wasn't sure what my feelings for her meant. Is this what it meant to have a best friend? Were you supposed to want to kiss your best friend? I liked Melita, and I liked the way I felt when she was around. But I was also confused. I wished I had someone to talk to about all this. Someone who understood. I wasn't sure I could talk to Melita about it. Not yet. I didn't know what I would say. I didn't know if she felt the same way.

"Phoebe?" The voice startled me. I must have fallen asleep.

I opened my eyes and sat up in the hay. I had forgotten where I was. The triplets stood there, and although they didn't run away, they huddled together in a circle. Michael's curly head bobbed over the door.

"I still can't believe she had triplets," he said. "No wonder she was so fat. They're good-looking kids, though."

"Mmm." I was discombobulated.

"Nice haircut," he said.

I rubbed my eyes. "Really?"

"Makes you look grown-up. Mind if I join you in there?"

I nodded, then I shook my head. I meant yes he could come in, no I didn't mind. Michael understood, because he unlatched the door and walked in. The triplets didn't run away. They were getting used to human company. They came over to him and sucked on his fingers trying to get milk.

"Have you named them yet?" he asked.

I pointed them out. "Jasmine. Tulip. Rosebud. But I call this one Noodles." I patted Noodles on her back. "Because she still wobbles."

"Like wet noodles."

I didn't feel like talking, but I also didn't want Michael to leave, so I tried to think of something to say. "We'll probably have to go back to Rosebud once she walks better." Being this close to Michael suddenly made me nervous. He was supposed to be my prince, but I wasn't so sure anymore.

"Are you okay, Phoeb?" Michael said. "You seem a little distracted."

"I do?" I said.

Michael tousled my hair. "Yeah, you do, kiddo. Are you on this planet today? Did you lose some brain cells with your hair?"

"I'm being punished."

"And why's that?"

"For getting my hair cut."

"I like your hair short." Michael tousled it again. "It makes it fun to mess up. I like girls with short hair."

I perked up. "You do?"

"Yeah, don't you?"

I studied his face. What did he mean? "Michael, can I ask you something?"

"That sounds serious. Go ahead. Ask me anything."

"What do you think of Melita?"

"Melita. Hmm." He paused. "I don't know her that well. But she seems nice. Spunky. A little wild. Maybe a little dangerous."

"What do you mean?"

"She has a bit of an attitude. But I really can't say. Maybe I'm just not used to city girls, even though my sister lives there and all."

"Your sister lives in New York? Have you ever been there?"

"Just once. I'd like to go again, though."

"What's it like?"

"Big. Lots of people, buildings, things going on. It's exciting. I dunno. It's hard to describe."

"I want to go to New York," I said, surprising myself. "I bet it's a good place to take photographs."

Michael nodded. "Yeah, it would be."

There was silence for a minute, and then I said, "Melita's mother tried to kill herself. She's in a clinic. That's why Melita is staying here."

Michael shook his head. "That's rough. Really rough."

"I didn't like her at first, but now we're really close."

"Well, that's good. You need friends, Phoebe. And I bet she does, too."

I wanted to say more, but I didn't know how to phrase it. What would I say? *Oh, and I think about kissing her and might be in love with her?* Not so long ago I had wanted to kiss Michael.

Suddenly I decided to try something. Without thinking, I flung my arms around Michael's neck and mushed my lips onto his.

"Mmph," he mumbled in surprise. He pried my arms off and moved away from me with wide eyes. "Phoebe. Phoebe. Stop."

I sat back. He didn't taste like strawberries. He tasted

like cheese. It wasn't bad cheese. For some reason, this made me smile.

"What was that about?" he asked.

"Nothing," I said, moving away from him.

"You know I think you're a great kid, Phoebe. Really great. But—"

"It's okay, Michael. I just wanted to see, that's all."

"See what? If you could shock the daylights out of me?"

"To see what it's like to kiss a boy on the lips."

"Oh. That. And?"

"Not bad."

Now Michael laughed. "Well it helps if you like the guy. A lot. And if he's closer to your age."

"Thanks," I said. "You helped." I looked at him. I had dared to kiss him on the lips and I was living to tell about it. It was a nice kiss, but not that special. It wasn't like kissing Melita. Maybe he wasn't my prince charming after all. I felt like I had just grown up about a hundred years in one second, but I also felt more confused than ever.

"You're welcome. I guess," Michael said.

"Can we keep this a secret?" I asked. "It won't happen again." Now I was embarrassed.

"It's okay, Phoebe. I'll never tell," he said.

I got up and tousled his hair. "You're a great guy, Michael. Really great, but . . ."

And I left him there a bit dazed, shaking his head.

10

A few days later Dad promised we could go shopping for a new pair of sneakers. My old ones were pinching my toes. "Do your chores and we'll go to town later," he'd said when I showed him my sneakers. I was excited at the thought of getting a brand-new, squeaky-clean pair and for once not having to put up with Phil's hand-me-downs. And maybe, if I played my cards right, and if Reny's sold them, I could get a pair of open-toe city shoes with a big heel. Melita could help me pick them out.

The air, as I skipped down the path from the barn, was warm and clean. A thunderstorm the night before had cleared out the mugginess, and everything was dewy and fresh. I swung the milk pail, careful not to spill any, and hummed a Patsy Cline tune.

I stopped short at the driveway. A black sedan was parked next to the truck. With New York license plates.

I opened the entryway door. It was no use yelling, because unless someone was in the backroom, you couldn't be heard, but I yelled anyway as I walked through to the kitchen. "Hey! Who's here?"

Dad was leaning against the sink filling the teakettle. A woman sat in one of the chairs facing him.

"Phoebe," Dad said, "this is Melita's mother. Gerelyn Forester."

The woman turned around, stretched out a long bare arm, and said, "I've heard so much about you, Phoebe. It's a pleasure to meet you."

She was dressed in a black sleeveless dress, more traditional than what Melita would wear, and she had straight dark hair that fell past her shoulders and ruby-red lips against pale white skin. She was as thin and fragile as my china doll. I was surprised to see how different she was from what I'd expected. This was the same woman who had dumped all the food on the couch, who sang too loud at the wrong times, and who cried for days on end. The same woman who had tried to kill herself.

Gerelyn smiled at me, waiting for a response. I stared back. From the way Melita had talked, I had pictured her as some sort of crazy, cackling witch, but except for all the black, she looked relatively normal. Her face was soft. She looked like Melita.

She spoke again. "You're all Melita talks about. It's so nice to see her make a friend. Thank you" — she turned to Dad — "both of you, for taking such good care of my little pumpkin. I don't know what I'd have done without you."

"We've loved having Melita. She's been no problem at all," Dad said.

"That's good to hear. Sometimes she can be a handful," Gerelyn said. "And it's been so helpful for me to have this time. I finally feel good. I'm ready to make a fresh start."

"We're just glad you're getting some help now, Gerelyn. Carol would be, too." Dad's face got sad. It always does when he mentions my mother's name, which is probably why he almost never says it.

"I still miss her. I can't believe it's been ten years," Gerelyn said.

"Eleven," Dad said.

"And our kids are all grown-up now." Gerelyn looked at me and smiled.

No one said anything for a moment. I was still trying to figure out what was going on. "You were supposed to be gone all summer," I blurted.

"Manners, Phoebe." Dad shot me his look. "Is that how you talk to an adult?"

"Sorry, Mrs. Forester."

"Please call me Gerelyn, Phoebe. And that's quite all right. I guess Melita didn't tell you. But I am better now. And I've missed Mellie so much. We're going back to New York. I'm going to restart my career. My agent thinks he can get some stage work for me."

"But Melita likes it here," I said. "She doesn't want to go."

"Phoebe, if you can't say something nice, then don't say anything." This from Dad again. Then to Gerelyn, "You'll spend the night, I hope. I don't think Melita has packed or anything, and it's a long drive back. We'd love to have you."

I couldn't believe they were going on as if everything was okay. As if nothing had happened. As if things would just automatically go back to the way they were. Before Melita.

"Phoebe, maybe you could go wake Melita up and tell her her mother is here," Dad suggested. "I know you two will miss each other, so maybe we can plan a nice dinner tonight."

A nice dinner? Was he kidding? Did he think a nice dinner would solve everything?

And then, as if on cue, Melita herself appeared, rubbing her eyes and looking confused. Her hair wasn't gelled, so her bangs fell softly over her eyebrows.

"Oh, Mellie-pumpkin!" Gerelyn jumped up and threw her arms around her daughter. "I have missed you *soooo* much."

"Hi, Mom," she said.

"Why didn't you tell the Sharps I was coming to get you, sweetie? They're so surprised to see me. I told you last week I was ready to leave the clinic."

"I know, Mom. I just wanted to be sure before I told anyone."

"Well, here I am, pumpkin pie. And one hundred percent better. You have a well and happy mother again."

"I'm glad for you, Mom." Her voice sounded sarcastic.

"We'll leave in the morning. That'll give you some time to pack up and say goodbye."

"Do you want to show your mom around the farm, Melita?" Dad asked.

"Oh, sweetie." Gerelyn finally let go of Melita. "I'd love to see the farm. Why don't you get dressed and show me some of your favorite places?"

Melita went upstairs, leaving me alone with Dad and Gerelyn as they reminisced about college and how long it'd been since they'd seen each other. I waited around to see if they would say anything else about my mother, but when it didn't seem like they were going to, I slipped upstairs. "What's going on?" I asked Melita in her room. She was brushing her hair.

"I guess I have to go back home."

"Well, you could've told me."

"I just never know for sure if what Mom says is actually going to happen. She could say she's coming and then cancel at the last minute. I didn't want to tell anyone till I was sure."

"I guess you're sure now," I said. "Why do you want to live with her anyway, if you're never sure?"

"Phoebe." Melita turned to face me. "She's my mother. I have to go back with her. I want to go back with her."

I wanted to tell her not to go. But that felt even more mean-spirited and selfish. She was right. Family is family. And Gerelyn was all Melita had.

"I'll miss you, Phoebe, and the farm. I was just starting to like it here, even with all the mosquitoes and gross stuff. But if I missed everything I left behind, I'd be nothing but a big ball of missing. It's time for a change, a new start."

"That's what your mother always says," I reminded her.

"Well, she says it because it's true." She went back to fixing her hair.

"What about the show?" I said. "We have the costumes almost all ready."

"You can do it without me."

"No. You're the one who knows how to do it," I said. I was whining, but I didn't care. "I can't do it alone." I practically whispered this last bit. My throat burned with backed-up tears.

"There's nothing to it. Just get another person, adver-

81

tise, get dressed, and walk down the aisle."

"But I don't know anyone." The tears pushed their way to the front. I couldn't just make another friend. I didn't want to make another friend. I wanted Melita.

"Be a little more outgoing, Phoebe. There are people around. What about that girl, Beth?"

I didn't know why Melita was being so cold. This wasn't like the Melita I knew at all. This was some stranger.

"Now if you'll excuse me." Melita fiddled with her hair some more, figuring out what to do with it. "I have to get dressed and packed, and you're being a pest."

"And you're being mean!" I yelled as I stormed across the hall to my room. I slammed the door as hard as I could and stood by Fred's cage. Fred immediately hid. I tapped his shell lightly, then harder.

"Hey, Fred," I said. "I'm a pest." No response. "Come out, Fred! I'm talking to you!" But Fred didn't budge. "At least you have a shell to crawl into. Feel lucky."

The sun was still shining, brighter than ever, but I no longer had the sense of joy I had felt only a little while ago. I sat down on the edge of my bed and kicked off my tight sneakers. *Damn them,* I thought. *Damn Gerelyn. Damn Dad. And damn Melita, too.*

11

The following morning Melita and Gerelyn drove away in the black sedan. Melita tried to be friendly, and she said goodbye and hugged me, but I couldn't respond. She was acting like this was all just fine. That we'd never see each other again and that was that. She said she'd e-mail, but that wasn't the same thing at all. I couldn't tell her how I felt. Every time I wanted to talk, something happened. You wouldn't think that on a farm there could be so many interruptions, but there were. And now she was gone and I'd never figure it out. I felt like I'd just lost my best friend. I had.

A week passed. I tried reading the books I'd planned to, but they didn't hold my interest. I would read the words but couldn't get lost in them like I wanted to. Without Melita, the farm suddenly seemed boring. Petunia and the triplets couldn't talk back to me. I took pictures, but even that wasn't satisfying. My useless camera was bothering me more than ever. I walked around moping all the time. Even Phil noticed and cleared the table several times when it wasn't even his turn.

One day I gathered all the stuff for the fairy tale outfits, carefully folded them, and placed them back in the trunk.

I just didn't see myself doing all this without Melita.

The raspberries ripened, and all I thought about was how Melita would have complained about the prickers and get all scratched up like I always do, but then we'd eat them and smile at their sweet taste. Maybe even feed them to each other Cleopatra-style. I imagined her holding them above my head, like grapes. "Open wide," she'd say and gingerly place a berry in my mouth.

I took a bucket out to the patch and started filling it. Plop. Plip. Plop. I picked the largest berry and bit down on it. The juice filled my mouth. It was a luscious, perfect red raspberry. I heard Melita's bell-like laugh almost as clearly as if she were there, and then a rustle in the briars. I called her name. Silence. Then all of a sudden a pheasant ruffled its feathers and rose up in front of me.

I jumped in surprise and fell right into a thicket of berries complete with prickers. The berries I had so laboriously chosen spilled on the ground. I groaned.

As the pheasant took flight, I shook my fist in the air and attempted to pick myself up. The prickers attached themselves to my T-shirt, not to mention my bare arms, and I had to pry myself loose. Melita would have thought this was a riot. She would have teased me until I laughed, and I would have made her help me pick up every berry. But Melita was gone. As suddenly as she had appeared in my life, she had disappeared. I knelt down and gathered fallen berries in my bucket but soon gave up and left the rest to rot.

I came into the house to find Dad on the phone. He smiled as he handed me the receiver.

"Hello?" I said.

"Hey, you!"

"Melita!" I put the berries down. Dad left the room.

"What's new? How're the triplets? I've been thinking about them," she said, as casually as if we had spoken yesterday.

"Standing and walking like they were born that way. I just picked some raspberries. Want some?" I didn't tell her about the pheasant, or the fall, or how I'd been thinking about her.

"Sounds delicious."

We chatted for a few minutes about the farm and the weather. Neither of us mentioned her leaving. We just picked up as though nothing had happened and we had always been friends.

"Did your father tell you?" Melita asked.

"Tell me what?"

"My mother asked if you could visit me in New York. They were just talking about it."

"Really?" I peered around the corner to see if Dad was in the living room, but he'd disappeared. "I can go?"

"Well, I don't know what the answer is yet. But my mom sounded pretty persuasive."

Gerelyn. I wondered how she was. Was she really all better like she'd said? I seemed to be the only one who really worried about her. Even Dad said now that she was on the right medication she'd be fine.

"Do you want to?" Melita was asking.

"See you in New York?"

"No, in Antarctica, silly."

New York City. I'd been to Portland (the biggest city in Maine) several times and Boston once when I was little, but New York was the biggest city of all.

"We can go to the flea markets in SoHo, Saks Fifth Avenue, the Empire State Building, the Statue of Liberty . . ." Melita went on and on listing everything she could think of in New York. Places that were just names and images to me, from I don't know where. Television, magazines, movies.

"I miss you," I suddenly said.

"Yeah, me too. I mean you."

"I'd love to come to New York."

"Fabulous, darling. I can't wait!"

"But, Mel?"

"Yeah? What?"

"Your mom . . . Is she . . . I mean, is it all right?"

"Oh." She laughed, a bit nervously I thought. "Yeah, she's doing great. Better than ever. Didn't you get my e-mail?"

"Yah, but . . ." I wasn't convinced.

"She really is, Phoeb. She's got a new agent who's getting her all sorts of auditions. She has a callback today for a show. And she can't wait to see you again. She wanted me to invite you here. She likes you."

Was it Gerelyn's idea, then, or Melita's? I wondered.

"You'd be surprised, Phoeb. She's like a new person. Aw, come on. It'll be my chance to show you where I'm from."

"I said I wanted to. I just wondered, that's all."

"Besides, we have the show to do!"

"In New York?"

"Sure, it's perfect. There couldn't be a better place. I

even know a space where we could have it. There's this café with a stage. I met the people who own it. I bet we could put it on there. Mom can get some of her friends to come. We already have the outfits. And you're right, Phoebe, you really shouldn't have to do it by yourself. This is a team effort. We could even get some other people to be in it so you won't have to be onstage so much."

Melita went on and on about the show and New York, how New York is the center of fashion and we'd be in the midst of it.

"And Phoebe?"

"Yah?"

"I've got some great news."

"What?" With Melita, "great news" could be anything from a new pair of shoes on sale to winning a trip around the world.

"There's someone I want you to meet. But you can only meet him in person, so get your butt down here. We've just got to convince your father. That'll have to be your job. Okay?"

My mind was stuck on the word *him*.

"Phoebe?"

"Okay," I said.

"Great! Then I'll talk to you as soon as you know, and we can make plans." She said goodbye. I held the phone for a few minutes before putting it down.

I found Dad outside weeding the garden. I asked him about New York.

"I'll have to think about it," he said.

"That's lame," I said. "What is there to think about?

Either I can go or not."

"Just hold your horses, Phoebe. I said I need to think about it."

"It's because of her mother, isn't it? But Melita said she's all better."

"It's not just that. Although I'll admit I have my reservations about Gerelyn."

"But she's one hundred percent better!" Now I was sounding like Melita. "You talked to her, didn't you? And she was Mom's friend. Don't you trust her?"

"Yes, but New York is a big city, Phoebe."

I gave him my most responsible look. "I will be very, very good. I promise. I really want to go."

"You haven't traveled much, though. You don't know about cities."

"And whose fault is that?" I raised my voice. He was making me mad. "You're the one who thinks I can't go anywhere. You keep me here supposedly protected from the big, bad world, but I don't even know what the world is all about. I have to learn sometime."

Dad sighed and wiped his cheek with a dirt-covered hand. "Maybe you're right," he said.

"And maybe," I went on, calmer now, "maybe the world isn't so bad as you think it is." I could hardly believe I was the one who was saying this. Me, the pessimist.

"Maybe." He sighed again and stared at the weeds in his hand before dumping them in a pile. "As long as you're here, Phoebe, why don't you help me do some weeding?"

I opened my mouth to protest but thought better of it,

and pulled a tiny sprout of weed from between the lettuce plants. I figured it was best to cooperate if I was trying to win permission.

"I really want to go, Dad. I am capable of going."

"I know, sweetie."

"I really miss Melita. A lot."

Dad stopped weeding and studied me. He does that sometimes as if he's trying to read my mind. I wouldn't be read, though.

"You didn't want her here at first," he said. "Remember?"

"I just didn't know her. I thought she was stupid because she'd never seen a goat or a horse before. But that's just 'cause she never had the chance. But now I know better. It's not her fault and she *is* smart. And I bet if I go to New York, I'll see lots of new things."

"I'm sure," he said.

"And she wants to put on this show," I said and tried to explain, though I was careful not to mention the clothes and material from my mother's trunk. I didn't think he'd be so keen on that. "She needs me to take the pictures. I might even learn something." This always gets him. And it worked, too. Dad laughed.

"You just might," he said, then added, "I'm not sure who would chaperone you."

"I don't need a chaperone! You've let me run all over here by myself, all my life."

"The city is different, Phoebe. There's crime. It can be dangerous. There's a lot you don't know."

"Well, Melita knows it."

"That's what I'm afraid of."

"You don't trust me!" I exclaimed, standing straight up.

"Now calm down, Phoebe. It's not that I don't trust you. That's not it at all. I, well, I just don't want you becoming materialistic, that's all."

"That's stupid," I pronounced. "I'm just me, Dad. You can't protect me forever."

He studied me again.

"Besides," I said, "going to New York is not going to change me. I'm not going to suddenly turn into glam girl and come back covered in tattoos. It will just give me more experiences so I can make better decisions."

Dad shook his head and smiled. "How'd you get to be so smart?"

I shrugged. "Smart father?"

He laughed. "I guess you've got me there."

"Then I can go?" I knew I was pushing it, but I could tell he was about to give in.

"There's the problem of how you'll get there."

"There's a bus," I said. "I can take it by myself. Melita did."

Dad frowned at that idea.

"I could ask Michael. He said he wanted to visit his sister. If Phil can feed Star for him, I'll bet he'll go."

"I'll think about it. It might be okay if you went with Michael."

"Yippee!"

"But only if he is going anyway and is willing to take you. I don't want you to beg him."

"I won't. I'll just ask."

"Well, then, maybe."

"Dad, you're the greatest!" I flung my arms around him,

and he gave me a quick pat on the back.

"We'll have to see what Michael says, first."

But I knew, with the toughest part of the battle won, I was as good as on my way to New York. All I needed to do was persuade Michael to actually go visit his sister. Piece of cake.

"Don't worry, Dad," I said. "Nothing's going to happen. I'll come back the same."

"You'd better," he said.

We heard Michael's truck rumble up the driveway. I gave Dad a pleading look. This was my chance.

"All right," he said. "Go on. I'm just about ready to quit here anyway."

I ran out of the garden and down the driveway to further hone my convincing skills.

City

12

The trip was long, but Michael had a CD player in his truck and we listened to music the whole way. He even got me to sing along to his rock music. I told him about our plan for the fashion show. He just looked at me and shook his head. "You're one interesting kid," he said. I suppose *interesting* is better than *cute* at any rate.

We got into the city at around six; it had taken us almost nine hours. We got a little lost driving through a sea of traffic and yellow taxicabs. Noise and pollution were everywhere, but there was so much to look at. Buildings—tall and narrow, short and wide, brick, concrete, and steel. People and shops along every sidewalk. Eventually Michael found the street where Melita lived—relatively quiet, narrow, tree-lined, with rows and rows of brick townhouses. The street was even narrower because of all the cars parked on both sides. There were no empty spaces.

"Why don't you hop out and get her," Michael said. "I'll wait right here."

The neighborhood was pretty. Quaint, even. Across the way a woman in a pale gray skirt suit was picking up her poodle's poop. I immediately thought of Bear being walked around a city. I don't think Bear's ever been on a leash, and I've certainly never picked up his poop with a plastic bag or any other implement. Two clean-cut men in shorts walked by holding hands, laughing and animated. They said hello to me and I said hi back.

The door to Melita's building was massive and had iron railings across thick glass. I walked up the steep steps and rang the buzzer that said Forester. A muffled "hello" came over the intercom.

"It's Phoebe," I said. "My stuff's in the truck. Michael couldn't find a place to park."

I heard a lot of crackling and then something that sounded like "right there," or was it "fight fair"?

I turned around and smiled at Michael. The woman had finished picking up the poop and disappeared inside another brick building with a thick door. I guess that was all the walking the dog got to do that evening.

There was a click as the door opened, a squeal, and then arms around my neck. Melita turned me around and gave me a huge hug. All my anxiety melted into that hug. It felt so good to see her again. Nothing else mattered.

"I can't believe you're here! You're actually here!" She jumped up and down in her orange platform flip-flops.

"I'm here," I said.

It had been only two weeks since Melita left the farm, but it felt like months. She looked different. Her hair was pulled back into a mini-ponytail about the size of Lambchops's tail and she had a bright red stripe instead of purple. Her short skirt and skimpy tank top looked right in place.

I looked down at my scabby knees and Birkenstock sandals. I knew New York would be more fashionable, so I had chosen to wear my nicest pair of shorts and my favorite short-sleeved shirt, the white one with faux buttons and a big sailor collar. I never wore it at home because it would only get dirty. But next to Melita I still looked out of place and wished I had on something more citylike and cool.

Michael got out of the truck and came over to us with my extra-large duffle. It was stuffed with all our costumes.

"Thanks for bringing her here, Michael," Melita said.

"No problem. It was great to have the company." He carried my bag up the steps.

"Do you want to come in?" Melita asked.

"I'd love to, but I'm later than I thought and my sister was expecting me a while ago. I still have to get over to Brooklyn. Maybe on the way back?"

"Sure," Melita said.

Michael put his hand on my shoulder. "Be good, now, Phoebe. You've got my sister's cell phone number if you need anything?"

I nodded and felt the piece of paper with the number on it in my pocket.

"I'll give you a call Sunday before I come get you, okay? You sure you're all right?"

"Yes," I said. "Don't worry."

"I'm not worried. I just feel a little responsible having brought you here. You won't forget to call your father and let him know you're here?"

"First thing," I said. "I'll do it right now."

"I'll remind her," Melita said. "Don't worry."

"Is your mother around?" Michael asked.

"She's at a meeting, but she's going to meet us for dinner."

"Okay, then," Michael said, standing there, his curls bobbing up and down as he nodded. He walked back down the steps and got in his truck. "Call if you need anything, Phoebe. Anything at all."

"Okay," I said. "I'll be fine."

A car beeped behind him, and he pulled away, waving his hand out the window. My stomach lurched slightly. There went my link to home. Then I turned and smiled at Melita. Here was my link to the city.

Melita picked up my bag. "He's so protective of you."

"Yah, it's like having another dad all of a sudden," I said, rolling my eyes. Just what I needed.

"I think it's sweet."

I followed her inside. The heavy door clicked behind us. She led me to the elevator and pressed number four. "We're at the top," she said, wiping sweat from her forehead. "Welcome to August in the city."

I wanted to tell her more about the ride. How all the little towns slowly began to get bigger and bigger as we got closer to New York, until finally all you could see was a sea of buildings. When we got to New York we drove right through the middle of some of the slummiest places I had ever seen. Buildings that were falling down, garbage strewn along the streets, bums begging and sleeping in doorways. I was glad I was just watching through the window, though I also really wanted to take pictures of it all. The world seemed so big, and I wanted to take it all down for documentation, as if having a photograph of a limited section could somehow make it more tangible. I felt an odd connection with the things I saw, and I wanted to show them to everyone. People everywhere should know that life like this really does exist.

But at the same time, I also kept hearing Melita's word *him* on the phone. I wanted to ask her about it, but I also didn't. When the elevator stopped, Melita brought it up for me.

"I met a guy," she said. "Tomas." She pronounced it like 'Toe-mas.' "He's French. He plays guitar. I asked him to play for the show." She leaned over and said in a hushed voice, "He's gorgeous and he's sixteen. I have a huge crush."

My mouth formed an O as my heart sank to the bottom of my feet.

13

Melita fumbled with at least four different locks to get in and plopped my bag on the floor. "Want something to drink? Diet soda? Orange juice?"

"Just water," I said. My throat was parched, partly from the heat, but mostly from Melita's news. "With ice."

I looked around, trying to forget what Melita had just said. If I ignored it, maybe it would go away. The place was like a big loft, with a counter separating the kitchen from the living area. It was sparsely furnished, which made it appear open, but still it was smaller than I had expected for someone as rich as Gerelyn. The first thing I noticed was the gigantic picture window and the view of the street. The walls were bright white, and, except for a clock in the kitchen and one large bright painting in the living room, they were bare. I went over and examined the painting more closely. It was a collection of roundish abstract shapes weaving about in primary and secondary colors, green and blue and yellow and orange clouds all floating against a sea of purple, with a thin line of red trickling down from each shape as if the paint had dripped.

"Isn't that cool?" Melita said, handing me a tall glass of ice water.

I nodded. "Who did it?" I placed the cold glass against my forehead. Even though the apartment was air-conditioned, I still felt hot.

"Mom."

"She's an artist?"

"She painted a lot before I was born. Then her acting career took off and I guess she just stopped. Sometimes I wish she had decided to be an artist instead of an actress. I think it'd be a calmer life. She calls this piece *Life Lines*."

"Where is she?" I asked, glancing around.

"Who knows. Some meeting. She's always got something to do or somewhere to be. She used to be home all the time, and now she always has appointments. It's better this way. She's getting her life back together after . . ." Her voice trailed off.

I changed the subject. "What time is the play tonight?" The other surprise Melita had told me about was that her mom was taking us to see *Beauty and the Beast* on Broadway. Now that was some news I was excited about.

"It's not a play, it's a show," Melita said. "It starts at eight. We're going out to dinner first, and Mom's going to meet us at the restaurant."

"Oh. What time is it now?" I looked around for a place to sit. The only furniture was an overstuffed, stark-white couch, a straight-backed chair, and a coffee table. So different from home, where books and farming magazines and dust spilled over everything. I plunked myself down on the couch, hoping I wasn't getting dirt on it. It was so soft and huge I was instantly engulfed. I propped myself up with a pillow.

"It's almost five-thirty. I thought maybe you could meet Tomas before dinner, but it's too late now."

I tried to imagine Melita with a boyfriend. My head could not grasp it. She had flirted with Michael and even Phil, but that was different. They weren't serious. I felt betrayed, though there was really nothing to betray. As far as I knew, Melita just thought of us as friends. I wanted to pretend that nothing was different, that we could go on as we had at the farm, even though that was killing me, too. I didn't know which was worse, not knowing or her having a boyfriend. I bit my tongue. I could go on like this. I would just go with the flow. At least we were together.

I took a large drink of water and swallowed the tightness in my throat. "How did you meet him?" I asked.

"I started hanging out at the café where he works, and we just clicked. He has such a sexy accent and a ponytail." Melita tilted her head back dreamily, stretching her long neck.

"I thought long hair was out," I said, feeling my own short do.

"Not on guys it's not. On guys it's very in."

"Where have you gone on dates?" I wasn't sure I wanted to hear the answer.

"He hasn't actually asked me out yet, but he will. I can tell. He's smitten with me—you'll see."

"So, you haven't kissed?"

"Well, no, not actually. But we will."

I let out my breath and stared at Gerelyn's painting

again. This time I saw all sorts of monsters eating each other.

"Well, come on. We've got to get ready. Let me see what you brought to wear. You can borrow something of mine if you want. And Mom said we could each wear a piece of her jewelry."

The door at the back of the living room led to a whole separate area with a huge bathroom and two large bedrooms. We went into hers.

Melita pulled a flowing pale orange dress from the closet and held it up to me. "Try this," she commanded. I took off my shirt and quickly pulled the dress over my head, lost in the flows of fabric for a second. It fell just below my knees, covering my scrapes. I chose a simple gold chain from her mother's box and a pair of old clip-on earrings. Melita wore a short black dress, of course, fake diamond earrings, and a necklace to match.

After we dressed, Melita dabbed some mascara and lipstick on herself, then me.

"Just a little," she said. "So we look sophisticated but not overdone."

We stood side by side in front of the mirror admiring each other.

"You look great, Phoeb. You dress up well. I can't wait to do the fashion show, can you?"

I was growing less and less excited about the fashion show with each passing minute. I hadn't been that excited about it to begin with, and now it seemed silly. What was our reason for doing it, anyway? Originally it was to make money, but that seemed unlikely. I guess we were doing it for fun. That, and to change people's perceptions of the women in fairy tales, which was as good a reason as any.

Melita took my hand and squeezed it. "Hey," she said. "I am glad you're here, you know."

Her touch made everything a little better. Maybe it was the dress, maybe it was New York, but I believed her. The dress matched the color of my hair, and although it was a little loose in the front, it fit perfectly everywhere else. I don't know how to explain it, but at that moment I felt as if I could actually see myself getting older, more mature. Even if Melita had a boyfriend, couldn't we still be close? Besides, they hadn't even kissed.

"What's he like?" I asked. I didn't want to say his name.

Melita sighed. "He's a dream."

I tried to imagine what this sixteen-year-old French boy looked like, but all I could picture was Michael with long hair and an accent.

"When do you think you'll"—I swallowed. I didn't want to ask, but I was compelled—"kiss?" My throat was dry again and my heart beat uncomfortably as I waited for her answer.

Melita laughed. "You can't plan for things like that, silly. We have to go on a date first."

I shrugged. A part of me just refused to believe that Tomas even existed.

Melita looked at her watch. "We'd better get going or we'll be late."

Outside it was hot. Not just hot, but heavy, muggy, and dense. I took a deep breath. I hadn't noticed it in Michael's truck, but now the air stuck in my throat and made me cough. It was the kind of hot where even if you were naked, you would still be too hot, and all the people, noise, and traffic just made it hotter.

"They say this heat is supposed to break the day after tomorrow. It sure has been gross." Melita pulled her sunglasses down. "We'll just have to spend the days with air conditioners till it does. Mom gave us cab fare, but we can take the subway and save the money for spending at the flea markets later. It's an easy ride uptown."

"Isn't the subway dangerous?" All the horror stories I had ever heard of New York almost always included a subway.

"Nah. I ride it all the time. Don't tell Mom, though—she thinks I take taxis. Come on, this way."

Melita led me down one street and across another. I wanted to stop and look at everything, but I was afraid I'd lose her in the crowd, and then I'd be standing all alone in the middle of this giant city. There was so much to look at that I wouldn't know which way to turn.

The stench of urine on the subway stairs was so exaggerated in the heat that I had to hold my breath. You'd think I'd be used to strong odors from the farm, but I wasn't prepared for this. Maybe the fact that it was humans who lived like that made it worse. We passed a dirty, homeless man sitting on some newspapers. Next to him was a small, short-haired scrappy terrier so sound asleep, it almost looked dead. The man saw me staring and held out his hand. "Money for Pedro?" he asked.

I pulled two quarters from my pocket and gave them to him.

"You've got a pretty smile," he said. The dog raised its head and wagged its tail at me but didn't get up.

"Come on, Phoebe." Melita tugged my arm. "First thing you learn in a city is you don't dilly-dally."

"But the dog," I said.

"A lot of homeless people have dogs. It keeps them company. Besides, the dog looked loved and it certainly wasn't starving."

We walked down, down, down, to the center of the earth, which turned out to be a clammy, low-lit station with graffiti on the cement walls and snakelike trains winding their way in both directions, making a whirring, ear-piercing screech as they passed. It was too loud to talk anymore. An older, very obese woman sauntered slowly down the stairs. She had rolls of fat under her chin, and her ankles spilled over her wide-strapped sandals. She walked with a cane, and her daisy-print shift clung to her body with sweat. I tried to imagine how she must have looked when she was younger. What had she been like as a teenager? Was she married now? Was she a mother? A grandmother? A college-age Asian girl ran by her. Very pretty. Long straight hair and a tall lanky body. She wore practically nothing—low-rise shorts so short that she was all legs. A tank top so high that she was all stomach. There was a gold ring in her bellybutton and a yin-yang tattoo on her shoulder.

The subway train roared to a stop, and we crammed on. We found two seats together and grabbed them. I started counting piercings. Six people had multiple earrings, three had rings in their noses, one had a stud in his bottom lip, and several had belly rings. One guy with a mohawk had so many studs in his face it looked like chrome acne. They went all the way up each ear, along his eyebrows, a few in his forehead, one in the groove under his lip, and one in each of his nostrils. My jaw clenched with the thought of all that pain. I'm sure he had one in his tongue as well.

"Some people even have their nipples pierced," Melita shouted in my ear over the din, as if she'd read my mind. I kept my arms folded across my chest the rest of the way.

14

The restaurant had Indian rugs, chandeliers, and a single candle on every table. We got there before Gerelyn. The hostess led us to our seats, filled our wineglasses with sparkling water, and put a basket of puffy bread on the table. We ate almost all of it while we waited. Finally, after twenty minutes, Gerelyn came blustering in. She looked much better than the last time I had seen her. Although she was still thin, her cheeks flushed with a healthy glow. She was dressed in a simple white linen dress and sparkling earrings.

"I'm so sorry I'm late!" she said, a little too loud. "Have you ordered?"

"No, Mom. We were waiting for you."

"That's sweet," she said, sitting down and running her hand through the entire length of her hair. In spite of their different skin tone, eye color, and hair length, Melita and Gerelyn looked very much alike. The shape of their faces and the angle of their noses were just the same. And they both flailed their arms around when they were excited.

"You can get whatever you like, girls. They're especially known for their lamb dishes, though." Gerelyn fanned her arm across the table.

"Mom," Melita whined.

"What, dear?"

Melita rolled her eyes at her mother and let out a frustrated *tsk*. Gerelyn didn't get it. "What?"

"Phoebe lives on a farm." Melita drew out the word *farm* as if that explained everything.

"I know that." Gerelyn patted me on the hand, then turned back to Melita. "What are you trying to say, dear?"

"They slaughter their own sheep!"

Gerelyn laughed. "Oh, well, I think Phoebe knows that she doesn't have to order lamb if she doesn't want to. Don't you, Phoebe?"

I nodded. "Yes, Mrs. Forester."

"Oh, please don't call me that. It's Gerelyn, remember? You don't have to be so polite with me."

I felt shy around Gerelyn, but I liked her. On the farm she had seemed quiet and mostly excited to see Melita. Now she seemed more comfortable and poised. I wondered what she must have been like in college when she and my mom were friends. Were they friends like Melita and me?

All through dinner Gerelyn kept asking questions about the farm and Dad and Phil. I answered politely.

"Your hair is the same color as your mother's, you know that?" she said.

I nodded. That was about all I knew.

"Except hers was longer. God, she could spend hours doing things with her hair. She had some very elaborate creations. Tight French braids twisted up in the back, rings around her ears like Princess Leia in *Star Wars*. Even just down it looked great all curled around her face like a halo."

I leaned closer, hoping for more.

"Carol and I went through a lot together," Gerelyn mused. I was afraid she was going to leave it at that. I wanted specifics.

"Like what?" I asked.

"Oh, you don't know much about your mom, do you, honey?" Gerelyn put her hand on my elbow. "Roger was so in love with her that it must have just devastated him when she died. It devastated all of us, but him most of all. It's not really a surprise he hasn't remarried. He was in complete awe of her. He would have done anything for her."

Including forgetting about his kids when she died, I thought. Then I instantly felt guilty for thinking that.

"I met Carol for the first time in art class. She came stumbling in with a sketchpad about twice her size. She was so petite, but you forgot it because she had this presence. She walked right into an easel, and the whole thing, including herself, crashed to the floor. Everyone in the class was quiet. We didn't know whether to laugh or call an ambulance. Then she just stood up and made a performance out of it. She curtsied and said this was her planned entrance. I knew right then that I liked her."

So my mother was klutzy like me. But I doubt I would have made the smooth comeback she did. I'd probably just apologize and slink into a corner to stew in my embarrassment.

"She sounds fun," Melita said. "See, you've got a bit of performance glamour in you, Phoeb." She punched my arm lightheartedly. "I know you'll be a natural in the show."

"What show?" Gerelyn asked.

"We're doing a fashion show, Mom. We started it in Maine, and Phoebe brought all the outfits here. We're hoping to do it at this café in the East Village."

"It's a spinoff of modern fairy tale women," I said. I felt like I had to clarify it as more than just a fashion show, seeing as it went against all my tomboy instincts.

"That's a great idea," Gerelyn said. "No wonder you were so eager to see *Beauty*. I thought it was a little young for you, but now it makes sense. Let me know if I can be of any help for your show."

"Thanks, Mom, but I think we're pretty set. You can come, though, once we know what day it's going to be."

We ordered, and talk of my mother ended, but I had gotten more than ever before, so I was satisfied for the time being.

About halfway through the meal I got up the nerve to say something to Gerelyn about her painting. "I really like your art."

Gerelyn put down her fork and smiled. A warm smile. "Thank you, Phoebe." She put her hand on my shoulder so tenderly it was like an embrace.

"You should start painting again, Mom," Melita said. "Everyone loves that piece."

Gerelyn reached across the table and put her hand over Melita's. "Maybe I'd have done better as an artist. But it just wasn't for me. I couldn't spend that much time isolated in a studio. I need to be around people. You know that, sweetie. Keep your fingers crossed for this next audition. My agent thinks I've got a good chance."

"What are you auditioning for?" I asked.

Gerelyn turned to me. "A play off-Broadway. A lead part. I'm through with bit parts in TV commercials and film. Film stinks."

"What's bad about film?" I asked.

Both Gerelyn and Melita laughed. I looked from one to the other. Gerelyn's laugh was big and genuine, while Melita's was small and nervous.

"Film drives me crazy," Gerelyn said. "Literally."

"Oh, I see," I said, suddenly uncomfortable.

"She's just kidding," Melita said. Then to her mother, "You're not crazy, Mom."

"I know, hon. I know. You'll see tonight, Phoebe, how much more real and exciting theater is. Film is all stop and start and a lot of waiting around. Theater is immediate; it thrives on its audience. There's nothing else like it. Your mother knew that, too. She had such an artistic sense for live theater."

And when the meal was over and I was sitting in a red velvet seat in row F at a theater on Broadway listening to Beauty sing to her Beast, I suddenly knew what Gerelyn meant by real. It was spectacular in every way, and I swear my mouth hung open through the entire show. The lights, the costumes, the scenery, even the audience, were mesmerizing. Gerelyn was right. Movies are easy to get lost in, but this was so much more exciting because you knew the actors were living and breathing right on the stage. It was a fairy tale brought to life.

After the finale, the whole audience stood up and

clapped, and some people even whistled and called out. Gerelyn put her arm around me and whispered, "I loved it, didn't you?"

I nodded. "There's nothing like theater," I said. I thanked her over and over for taking me.

"What did you think of Beauty's outfits?" Melita asked in the taxi ride home.

"They were beautiful, but pretty traditional," I said. Beauty wore long, elegant dresses with lots of puff and lace.

"I think our outfits are much better," Melita said.

We weren't doing *Beauty and the Beast*, but our Sleeping Beauty outfit was a long, low-cut dress made of layer upon layer of transparent beige cotton. There were so many layers that you couldn't quite see through it, though there were hints. The idea was that each layer represented a year that she was asleep.

By the time we got home and ready for bed, and I'd called Dad to let him know I was safe, not even traffic and sirens could keep me awake. I crawled onto the pull-out mattress next to Melita's bed. I was glad I was so tired, because I had a sinking feeling Melita wanted to tell me all over again how wonderful Tomas was, and I wasn't up for hearing it. I just wanted to sleep next to her, both of us breathing peacefully.

15

The traffic woke me in the early morning. Melita was still asleep, so I crept out of bed as quietly as I could and went to the bathroom. Funny how Gerelyn had so much more money than Dad did, and yet she didn't have a guest room. I guess that's the difference between New York and Maine. I saw Gerelyn at the kitchen table as I headed back. She was just sitting there in her bathrobe, holding a cup of coffee and staring into it. I watched her for a minute. I didn't know if I should say something to her or not. I decided not to and started to walk by.

She must have heard me, though, because she looked up and said, "Phoebe, dear. Good morning."

"Morning."

"Here, come sit and keep me company." She patted the chair next to her. "Mellie's always been a late sleeper. Ever since she was born. Always slept straight through the nights. How'd you sleep?"

"Fine, though I'm not used to all the noise," I replied as I sat down and folded my hands in my lap. We sat in silence for a moment. "I really enjoyed the show last night."

"I'm so glad. Can I get you some coffee?"

"Uh, no. Thanks." But she had already gotten up and poured me a cup from the coffeemaker on the counter.

"Do you take milk? Sugar?"

"Um, both, I guess." She poured some milk into the cup and brought it to the table. She placed it in front of me and moved the sugar bowl next to it.

"Help yourself," she said and sat back down.

I stirred the coffee and lifted the cup to my nose. I had always loved the smell of coffee, but I'd never really thought about drinking it before. It always seemed like one of those adult things that eventually I would do. I guess I was becoming more of an adult, so why not start now? One cup couldn't hurt.

"You know, Phoebe," Gerelyn began, "I don't know if you realize this or not, but you've been a really good friend to Mellie."

I nodded and brought the cup to my mouth. I took a small sip. It was hot and bitter. I stirred in a spoonful of sugar and tasted it again. I put in two more spoonfuls and stirred again. The spoon clinked against the inside edges of the cup.

"Mel thinks the world of you. And whether you know it or not, you've helped her through a very rough time. She doesn't have a lot of friends. I think moving around so much is hard on her. I thought it'd be good, you know? Adventure. Travel. New experiences. But maybe I've been wrong. I'm going to try to do the right thing from now on. We're going to stay here. Melita likes it here, and I've always felt at home in Manhattan. Know what I mean?"

I nodded and blew on my coffee to cool it down. I took another sip. This time it tasted pretty good.

"Mellie needs some stable friends. I hope you two will always stay in touch."

"We will."

"I want to repay you," Gerelyn said. I took another sip of coffee and waited. "I would like to buy you something special. Is there anything you want?"

"No," I said automatically. "You don't have to get me anything. Really. Letting me stay here, dinner last night, and the show . . ."

"I insist. I want to get you something. Isn't there anything you want? A pair of earrings, a new outfit?"

I shook my head.

"Don't worry about the money," she said. "Think of something you wouldn't necessarily get on your own."

She really did seem to want to buy me something. I wondered how I would explain a gift to Dad. He had had a hard enough time letting me stay there without paying Gerelyn. He was funny that way. He would go out of his way to do things, like let Melita stay with us and not accept money, but for him to let someone else do something for him, forget it. And he didn't like his kids to accept handouts, either. But why couldn't I accept a gift? Gerelyn was offering, and it would be rude not to accept. I thought about what I might want. Clothes and jewelry were fun, but I didn't really need them. No, if Gerelyn was going to buy me a gift, I wanted it to be something I could really use. Suddenly it dawned on me. It made perfect sense.

"A new camera," I said.

"A camera?" Gerelyn repeated. "Are you sure?"

"I like to take photographs. All I have is an Instamatic.

I'm saving for a darkroom."

"Okay. We'll get you a camera, then." She laughed and looked a bit more relaxed. "We'll get you a great camera so you can become a great photographer."

"Thank you," I said. Already I was seeing what I wanted to photograph. Everything there in the city: the run-down buildings, the homeless people in the streets, the flower gardens and gates of the brick townhouses on Gerelyn's street, Times Square where we went to see the play, the children playing basketball in the fenced-in lots. My mind wandered to the farm: Petunia and the triplets, the cats dashing through the barn, the sheep in their pasture, the dew on the grass first thing in the morning, or in winter the way the icicles drip off the long-fingered branches of the bare apple trees.

"There's a good camera shop not far from here. We can go tomorrow morning," Gerelyn said, interrupting my daydream.

I could take a picture of her, the way she looked now, with no makeup and her hair black as night cascading around her face and over her shoulders. She held her coffee cup between her hands, poised in midair.

"What's happening tomorrow morning?" Melita appeared in the doorway in her oversize nightshirt and her hair sticking up in all directions.

"I'm going to buy Phoebe a camera. Won't that be nice?"

Melita looked at her mother, then at me, then back to her mother. Without a word, she turned around and left. I heard her go into the bathroom and turn on the faucet.

"Someone got up on the wrong side," Gerelyn said.

"Maybe she's worried about Tomas," I said.

"Who?" Gerelyn asked.

Uh-oh. Maybe Gerelyn didn't know about Tomas. Melita hadn't told me it was a secret.

"Tomas?" I said softly, testing the name. "The guy at the café who's going to play guitar at our fashion show."

"I don't know all her friends. You're the only one she's ever talked about. But then I guess I don't keep track of her all the time." She sighed.

I shrugged. I wondered why Melita would keep Tomas a secret from Gerelyn. Would Gerelyn disapprove because he was older? Or because he was foreign? Would Melita be mad at me for blowing her cover? Gerelyn didn't seem too upset, so maybe it would be okay.

Gerelyn and I sat in silence listening to Melita in the bathroom. When she emerged again, her hair was wetted flat against her head and her face was splashed with water. I tried to detect some trace of emotion in her face, but I couldn't tell anything.

And then Gerelyn asked the inevitable. "Who is Tomas, pumpkin?"

Melita glared at me. "You told," she said.

I fumbled with my words. "I . . . I didn't know . . . I didn't mean to."

"Is he a new friend? A special friend?" Gerelyn smiled. Melita rolled her eyes. Gerelyn kept talking. "I'm not mad, I just want to know, that's all. I don't like your keeping secrets from me. And I'd like to meet him, of course. Where's he from?"

Melita let out an exasperated sigh. "You never cared before, Mom."

"Honey, I've always cared. It's just that I'm trying to express it better now. I want to know. You don't have to get angry. We can talk about things calmly."

Gerelyn's calmness was almost too much. I could see a fire burning under Melita. I remembered she told me that since her mother had gotten back from the clinic, she was supposed to avoid conflict.

"I'm *sick* of doing everything *calmly!*" Melita suddenly yelled. "I don't have to tell you everything I do. It's not like you really care or anything. I can't stand it!" She took a deep breath and stormed out of the kitchen, slamming her bedroom door and leaving Gerelyn and me speechless.

I stared into my coffee cup and concentrated on the little ridge of milk bubbles around the edge. Gerelyn hiccupped. I didn't want to look at her. Her breath came in short, quick gasps.

She whispered something so softly I could barely hear her. It sounded like "It's not fair."

In spite of myself I looked up. Her face was wet with tears, which glimmered in the sunlight and gave her an eerie glow.

"Gerelyn?" No answer. I wanted to tell her it was okay, to make her feel better. I raised my hand and let it rest on the table near her. "Gerelyn?" I repeated.

She looked at me and laughed uneasily.

"I bet you never yell at your father, do you, Phoebe? The doctors said, 'Be calm, don't get excited, remain rational.' Well, I'm trying. But it's not easy, you know? She's too much like me, or like I was."

She was talking more to herself than to me. Or maybe she thought I was somebody else, and not just thirteen-year-old Phoebe Sharp, best friend, or maybe now former best friend, of her daughter, the one who had a crush on that same daughter.

"My dad and I argue sometimes," I said. I don't think she heard me. "Gerelyn? I'm going to see if Melita's okay." My chair scraped unusually loudly against the tile floor as I pushed it back. Gerelyn put her hand on my shoulder. Her fingers felt like icicles. I shivered.

"That's good," she said. "Go talk to her. She loves you, you know. I think it's better you talk to her. She'll listen to you. Tell her I'm not mad, though, will you? I just want to be a good mother."

We stood up at the same time. "I need to rest now. But I won't forget your camera, Phoebe," Gerelyn said. Then we went in opposite directions. I waited until she had closed the door to her bedroom before I knocked on Melita's.

"Go away!" said a muffled voice.

"It's me," I said. "Can I come in?"

"No."

"Melita, I didn't know I wasn't supposed to tell. Honest, I didn't. And I wouldn't have, either, if you'd told me not to."

"I don't want to hear it" was the reply.

"I'm sorry, Melita. Let me in. I have to get dressed."

There was no response. I was about to knock again when I heard a thump—she must have jumped off her bed—then padding sounds closer to the door. She opened it wide, looked at me for a second, then scuffed her way

117

back to the bed and pulled the covers over her head.

"Just get your stuff and leave," she said.

"Where am I supposed to go?" I walked in and shut the door. "I have to stay here till next week."

"Well, I don't want to talk to you then."

"Melita, you're blowing this way out of proportion. Your mom's not mad at all. She seems so understanding."

No word from the blanket.

"Why are you so upset?" I asked.

"You wouldn't understand," came the muffled reply.

I sat down on the floor and hugged my knees. "Try me," I dared her.

She pulled the covers down and stared at me through the tears streaming down her face. She was looking at me so intently it made me uncomfortable. The silence was awkward and the room suddenly hot.

"Come here," she finally whispered.

I went over to the bed and sat down on the edge beside her.

"Lie down," she commanded.

I did. I stretched my arm out and tried to comfort her by patting her hair. It was silk between my fingers.

"Are you in love with Tomas?" I asked.

"I just met him. We haven't even been out yet." She sighed. "But I think I could fall in love with him if I wanted to."

I propped myself up on my elbows and stared down into her face. "Let's pretend," I said. "Like we used to." I wanted to keep talking. I wanted to say, *Before you had some guy you might fall in love with, when you needed to practice. Now you don't need to anymore. You have the real thing. Or at least you will.* I wanted to let her know how much she meant to me. I put my hands on her face and kissed her on the lips. She didn't seem startled or upset. She smiled.

"Melita, you're my best friend," I said.

"You're mine, too," she said.

"I've never had a friend like this before," I said.

"Me neither."

"I've never felt like this before."

"Me neither."

I could hear both our hearts thumping. The air was thick but important. I touched Melita's elbow, her dainty, pointy, smooth, beautiful elbow. I slid my hand down her forearm, and our fingers met and locked. Her caramel fingers intertwined with my peach ones. We kept them clasped and stared at the ceiling fan as it went around and around.

"And best friends love each other," I said.

"Sure they do," she said.

But I didn't think she meant it the way I did. Not really. I didn't know exactly how I meant it, but there was something different about the way I loved her. I felt alive when I was with her. It excited me a little, saddened me a little, and frightened me a little, too.

16

W e're off to buy a camera," Gerelyn announced to an elderly woman and her cocker spaniel. I smiled at the woman as we passed. Melita kept her head down and followed a few paces behind us. She hadn't said much to her mom. I didn't quite know what was going on between them, but I guessed Melita still had some forgiving to do. Though I could see how having Gerelyn for a mother could be frustrating. Her intentions were good, but her moods were unpredictable. She acted like everything was fine now, even though Melita had hardly spoken to her since the day before.

The birds were chirping a morning song from their perches in the maple trees that lined the sidewalks. Didn't they know this was a city? *Why don't you all fly to the country?* I wanted to yell, and point them in the right direction. But they seemed content, making their happy racket. Maybe they just got used to it like the people did. After all, they had the sky above them and could fly anywhere they wanted. Maybe some of these very birds flew over Plattville.

Once we got to the main street, the birds and the

flowers were replaced by traffic and construction. The neighborhood atmosphere changed to shops, restaurants, and crowds of rushing people.

We walked a long way, passing all sorts of people lined up on the sidewalk selling things: art, jewelry, headbands, handbags, watches, sunglasses, old books, record albums, tapes and CDs, clothing, even old shoes that looked like they were found in the garbage. A strong smell of incense wafted from all directions. There were people of all types: old, young, some with orange and purple hair, others clad in leather, and some wearing hardly anything at all, covered in tattoos. Voices, music, odors, and colors, were everywhere.

"And this is still morning," Gerelyn said when I commented on all the activity. "Wait till you see it at night. That's when the real weirdoes come out."

We walked some more, and finally Gerelyn stopped in front of an electronics and video store.

"Here we are," she said. "I've heard good recommendations for this place. They say it's the best camera shop in the Village."

"Can I help you, ladies?" a young salesman asked after we'd been looking around for a few minutes. There was such a variety of cameras and accessories, from small compact devices to huge, cumbersome attachable lenses.

"We're looking for a camera for this young lady," Gerelyn said. "Something good quality."

The salesman stared at Gerelyn. She was hard not to stare at, with her striking elegance, even first thing in the morning. "Okay, ma'am. Digital or not?"

"Not," I said.

He took us over to a glass cabinet and laid out several cameras.

Gerelyn picked one up, an Olympus 35 mm with a zoom lens. "Now, there's a nice-looking camera," she said.

I couldn't tell for sure, but it looked like she winked at the salesman. Melita was on the other side of the shop, so I know she hadn't seen it. He looked about twenty-five. He had short dark hair and deep black eyes. He smelled of after-shave. I think he was Italian. He blushed and smiled at Gerelyn, but he wouldn't look her in the eye. Gerelyn put the camera down and leaned over to pick up another one. As she did so, her hand brushed against his arm. He backed away and almost dropped a camera.

"Oh, I'm so sorry," Gerelyn said in a thick, syrupy voice that seemed to lure him back again. "What do you think, Phoebe?" she asked.

I studied the camera. I held the Olympus in my hands and looked through the lens at the salesman. I backed up so that both he and Gerelyn could fit in my view. Gerelyn leaned over the counter, delicately balanced on her thin elbows. She crossed one leg behind the other. The salesman kept his eyes on the counter, as if embarrassed that I would take a picture of him. I pressed the zoom button and watched Gerelyn fill the lens. My mother's best friend. My best friend's mother.

I turned around, still looking through the camera lens, and found Melita. Her back was turned to me as she handled some picture frames. They all had display photos in them—one of a dog and several with babies or fields of flowers or both. She picked up a family portrait: about ten people all crammed together, from elderly grandparents to toddlers in diapers on their parents' laps. I played with the zoom, going in and out. Close and far. Big and little. Face and body.

"Hey, Melita!" I pretended to take her picture as she turned around. She stuck out her tongue and wrinkled her nose, then turned back to the display.

"I like this camera," I said to Gerelyn and the salesman.

"Good choice," he said. "Compact, but it does everything. And it takes swell pictures."

"Swell!" Gerelyn repeated. She leaned closer to the salesman. From his point of view, I'm sure he could see right down her shirt. I could see her cleavage and the lace of her bra, and I was only at her side. But she wasn't embarrassed or anything. It was as if she knew he could see, but she didn't mind. It was sexy. Everything about Gerelyn was sexy. She could get away with it because she was so beautiful. Beautiful and delicate in body and mind. I wondered what would happen if I leaned over like that. First of all, there wasn't much to see, and second, I'd probably lean so far I'd fall right through the glass countertop. I didn't try.

"You want that one, Phoebe? Are you sure?" Gerelyn stood up straight and faced me. Her voice was louder now, back to normal.

I nodded.

She leaned over the counter again and whispered so the salesman was forced to move close to her to hear. "We'll take it."

I held up the camera and focused on the little beads of

sweat on the salesman's forehead.

"Throw in some film, too," Gerelyn said. She rummaged through her bag for her wallet while the salesman showed me how to load it.

"You're all set now," he said and actually smiled. "Enjoy it."

"I will," I said.

He rang us up at the register. I gasped when I saw the amount. Gerelyn handed over a credit card. "Don't worry about the cost. This is my gift to you."

"Can we go now?" Melita whined, joining us at the register. Was she mad because her mother was spending so much on me?

"Thank you," I said as soon as we were outside. I hurried to keep alongside Gerelyn's long strides. She took my arm and patted the back of my hand.

"You're welcome, dear."

She stopped and waited for Melita to catch up with us. She linked her other arm in Melita's.

"My girls," she said.

We walked along, Gerelyn in the middle, me right next to her, Melita pulling a little behind. For a second I pretended Gerelyn was my mother and this was what it was like to link arms and walk down the street with a mom. People stared at us as we walked, and when I got a glimpse of our reflection in a shop window I saw why. It was ridiculous for me to think that I could be Gerelyn's natural daughter. We were an odd sight. Two black-haired beauties, one with porcelain skin, the other with creamy brown skin. And me, all pinkish with freckles and fire engine hair.

"Why don't you take your first picture of Mellie and me?" Gerelyn said, slowing her gait.

"Okay," I said.

The two of them stood next to a parking meter. Gerelyn put her arm around Melita and bent her head as if she were about to kiss her on the cheek. She held that pose, her lips puckered a millimeter away from Melita, while I focused.

"Hurry up," Melita demanded.

I got the picture clear and pressed the shutter. I liked the way it sounded, as if a lot of mechanical activity was going on. Not just a simple click like my old one.

Melita squirmed away from her mother's clutches. "It's too hot to have you pawing all over me, Mom. Don't you have to be somewhere now?"

"Oh, gosh, that's right," Gerelyn said, glancing at her watch. "I have a lunch date."

"Figures," Melita said under her breath.

"Melita, I don't deserve that. You know I'm trying." She looked at me apologetically. "Are you girls all set for the afternoon?"

"Yeah, Mom. Don't worry. We can take care of ourselves."

"I'm not worried about you, hon. But remember, Phoebe isn't as familiar with the city as you are, so be careful."

"Yeah, yeah," Melita mumbled.

Gerelyn hailed a cab. "I'll see you back at the apartment then? Bring Tomas by for dinner if you want. I'd like to meet him."

My heart sank.

"Maybe," Melita said. *Maybe not,* I thought.

Gerelyn yelled from the cab's window, "Have a good afternoon, girls. I love you, Melita. You're my best daughter. Don't worry, I'll get you something special, too. I promise."

Melita and I stood in silence as we watched the yellow cab disappear into a sea of traffic.

17

I could no longer avoid it. It was time to meet *him*.

We walked through the park, and I slowed us down by taking pictures along the way.

"You'll really like Tomas. And the food at the café is delicious. Cardamom plum scones. Mmmm," Melita said as I took a picture of a little girl and her father out for a Saturday afternoon walk. I wondered if the father and mother were divorced and this was the father's weekend with his daughter. Or if the mother was dead and he was raising his daughter by himself. They looked like they were having fun. The girl chased a group of pigeons and squealed in delight as they flapped a few feet away and settled. She ran after them in circles, and the father ran after her, swung her up over his head, and then brought her back down and wrapped his arms around her in a bear hug. The girl giggled deliriously.

I focused my lens on a group of skateboarding punk rockers with grungy, spiked-up hair.

"Are you listening to me, Phoebe?"

"Yah, I heard you. Plum scones."

"Tomas has gorgeous hair. Thick and long."

"Oh," I said.

Melita went on and on about Tomas. His hair. His beautiful teeth. His French accent. His guitar playing. Tomas this. Tomas that. Blah blah blah. The more she talked about him, the more I wondered if he was real. He sounded too perfect to be true. He sounded like a prince. Like the guy who comes in at the end of the story and saves the princess but never has any personality. Like the guy I used to think Michael was, except for the personality part.

The café was crowded and looked like a fast food diner with wooden booths and 1960s posters of rock 'n' roll stars: the Beatles, Janis Joplin, Bob Dylan, and the Rolling Stones. There was a long counter with a row of stools.

"Sometimes they have live music here." Melita pointed to a small raised stage in the back with a table and chairs. "Tomas plays the guitar. This is where we can do the show. It's right near the bathroom, so we can change easily."

Clusters of people were hanging out, talking, laughing, and making gestures. One booth had six people crowded into it. Other people sat alone, reading or writing. A woman in a black macramé suit with her laptop looked like she was camped out for the day. There was a pleasant mix of laughter, conversation, whirring coffee machines, and jazz music. A general hubbub of social activity and happy people. I got the impression they were all doing something important. Or at least they thought they were. There was not one café in Plattville. The closest place to something even remotely like this was the Miss Pinenut Diner in the next town over.

We were definitely the youngest people there. Most of

them looked to be college-age. I tried to imagine Michael in a café like this, in his dirty jeans and messy hair. People here had messy hair and dirty jeans too, but it looked like it was a style and not because they had been shoveling horse manure. I wondered if my dad and mom and Gerelyn used to go to places like this when they were in college. I couldn't imagine Dad ever being this cool.

Behind the counter was a purple-lipped person; I wasn't sure if it was a boy or a girl. He or she had a blond buzz-cut and broad shoulders, but there was something feminine about the face. Small nose and delicate eyes. He/she wore a loose T-shirt and looked pretty flat-chested, so I couldn't tell from that. I studied her/his hands as they worked the fancy coffee machine. Small and nimble. Nails cut short. Boy? Maybe a nail biter. Must be a girl.

I looked around for a French prince charming. "Is he here?" I whispered.

Melita shushed me and pointed to a guy coming from the backroom.

I don't know if I'd go so far as to say he was gorgeous, but then, from the way Melita had been raving about him, I had high expectations. He was tall, lean, and had wide almond eyes; even from a distance I could tell he had thick lashes. Why do guys always get the thick eyelashes? And, yes, his hair was pulled back in a smooth ponytail. He brushed a loose strand behind his ear and waved to us.

"Melita." His voice was heavy with a French accent.

"Hi, Tomas," Melita said.

Tomas reached his arm over the counter and shook Melita's hand. "Nice to see you again," he said.

"You, too."

There was silence for a second. I stood there awkwardly.

The purple-lipped person was about to wait on us when Tomas broke in. "I will get this. Anything to drink, Melita? And for your friend?"

Melita introduced us, and Tomas put his hand out again. His hand was warm and he had a solid grip. "Coffee?" he asked, letting go.

I read the menu on the chalkboard behind the counter. There were almost a half-dozen ways of preparing coffee: cappuccino, mochaccino, espresso, latte, americano. And they all came in choices of single, double, light, decaf, hot, cold, with foam, without foam. While I was figuring out what each one was, Melita ordered an iced latte.

"I'll have an espresso," I said. It sounded sophisticated.

"Espresso's really strong," Melita said.

"I know. I like it that way."

"One iced latte, one espresso, coming right up," Tomas said. "I will bring them out when they are ready."

Melita and I slid into a booth near the window. "So?" Melita nudged me. "A babe, huh?"

"Yah, he seems nice."

"I'll say. I think he likes me."

When Tomas came over with our drinks, he scooted next to Melita in the booth. "Here you go. Two drinks for two beautiful ladies."

"Thanks, Tomas." Melita flipped her head back and opened her mouth in a half smile, half laugh, showing her clean, straight teeth.

"Are you a photographer, Phoebe?" Tomas pointed to my camera.

"I want to be." Suddenly I was very shy. I didn't know what to say to Tomas. I didn't want to like him.

"She's really good," Melita said.

"So tell me about your plan for this show and what you might like me to play," he said.

I let Melita explain it to him. How we came up with the idea to reinvent fairy tale women and how we found outfits for each of them.

"Sounds very postmodern and feminist," Tomas said, nodding his head the whole time.

"We were thinking you could play something kind of fresh and modern. Maybe some snappy jazz. Right, Phoebe?"

"Sure," I said.

"Or maybe classical. We want to show that these women have spunk and class. That no one messes with them," Melita said.

"Right," I said.

"We should get together and do a run-through," Melita suggested.

They made plans to meet the next day in the park. Great—was this like a date? Melita and Tomas chatted about the show and music. Tomas did seem genuinely interested in Melita; he kept staring into her eyes when he spoke. They went on and on, and I tuned them out to people-watch. I was very impressed with the way the girl/boy danced from customer to coffee machine to register, serving people in a single sweeping motion like some kind of café superhero.

"Phoebe?" Melita said my name and gestured to Tomas.

"Huh?"

"I said, how long are you in town for?" Tomas asked. I must not have heard him the first time. He had turned his attention to me, as if I were a side dish he had to deal with before getting to the main course.

"Five more days," I said. "I've been here two already."

"And what do you think of Manhattan?" he asked.

I thought of telling him that it was dirty, ugly, dangerous, and smelled of urine, but then I remembered Gerelyn's street with its pretty townhouses and gardens, the Broadway play, the plush restaurant, and the lights shimmering at Rockefeller Center when we rode by in the cab at night.

"A lot of people and buildings," I said finally.

"Yes, this city has lots of people running around. It is not very big, land wise, and that is why the buildings are built so high up. I have this theory. When you put so many people in a cramped space, you get all types, and whatever type they are gets magnified." He took a sip of his drink and went on. "If you are friendly, you get extra friendly, if you are mean, you get extra mean, and if you are weird, which most seem to be, you get extra weird."

"I see," I said. "So you're from France?"

"Yes, from Paris. But I have lived in New York since I was ten. My uncle owns this café."

"Your English is good," I said.

"Hey, Tomas!" the purple-lipped person called from the counter. "Need your help here."

Tomas smiled at us. "Be right there, Alex," he called back.

Alex. She even had one of those names that could go

either way. And her voice was low. Maybe she was a he.

Tomas stood, took Melita's hand, and kissed it. "Until tomorrow, then," he said.

Gag.

Then he did the same to me. I blushed.

Melita and I sat a while longer, finishing our coffees. I'll never order a double espresso again. It was so bitter I had to put four packets of sugar in and I still couldn't finish it. I could feel my pulse quickening and my face turning red. I guess I'm not so good with caffeine after all.

"Is Alex a boy or girl?" I whispered to Melita on our way out.

"Girl, silly. Look at her neck. No Adam's apple. And her eyes—that's how you can always tell. A woman's eyes are smoother around the edges."

"Oh," I said.

"I think we should ask Alex to be in the show. She'd look great in the Little Red Riding Hood outfit or Snow White."

I shrugged.

"It'd be helpful to have another person in costume, don't you think?"

"Yah, I guess so." I had agreed to appear as only one character, Rapunzel. Partly because it was difficult for me to think about appearing onstage and being looked at, but also because Rapunzel was the most appealing character to me. I could use my own braids, which we had tied together to make one long rope. When attached to my head, it fell down to my butt.

"With Tomas playing guitar and three of us in costume,

we'll have a great show." She whipped out her cell phone. "I'm going to ask Tomas right now to ask Alex."

I nodded. If I could only forget that Melita had a crush on Tomas, then I'd be much more excited. He wasn't so bad as a guy, but still, I was not looking forward to the next day. Not one iota.

18

The following morning Melita brought me to the neighborhood of SoHo. "There's some great shops," she said. "Maybe we can find some bargains."

The streets in SoHo were winding and narrow and filled with people. What was it Michael had told me? Eight million people lived in New York City, and only one and a half million lived in the entire state of Maine. No wonder I felt claustrophobic. But at the same time it was exhilarating to be around so many people—all going somewhere and doing something, even if it was nothing at all. I had never seen so many different people.

The storefronts were all different, too. Banners announcing fancy clothing boutiques, run-down clothing boutiques, shoe stores, bath stores, toy stores, hair salons, cafés, fancy restaurants, and art galleries. We went into one clothing store I thought was a thrift shop until I read the price tags.

"Two hundred and eighty dollars for a pair of ripped jeans!" I shouted to Melita over the booming dance music. "Are people crazy?"

"That's nothing!" she shouted back. "Look at this." She held up a dress covered with sequins and mouthed "one thousand dollars" to me.

The saleslady gave us the evil eye, so we left.

"I can't believe people spend that much money on clothes," I said, dodging the crowds and racing to keep up with Melita.

"You'd be surprised how easy it is," Melita said. "But over here is the place to go."

She led me down one narrow, car-jammed street and across another to an open lot where tables and booths were set up and people sold all sorts of things.

"We're bound to find some more things we can use for the show here," she said as she began milling through some of the items. One table had nothing but socks—all different colors and designs. Another table had T-shirts with art prints on them. A third table sold wool sweaters, and a fourth had leather wallets and bags.

I wandered over to a shoe table. The shoes looked like refurbished hand-me-downs. Some were really old-fashioned, with narrow heels and lots of laces, and others were more modern. I held up a pair of clear, rubber boots with snap closures.

"You'll need clean socks to wear these," I said.

Melita grabbed the boots from my hands and screamed, "We have got to get these!"

"You don't even know if they fit."

She held one against her own sandal. It looked big. If they were too big for her, they'd be huge for me.

"Doesn't matter," she said as she handed money to the seller and put the shoes in her shoulder bag. "They'll come in handy if Alex decides to join us. She's got big feet. She just has to say yes. I mean, why wouldn't she?"

I shrugged and didn't answer.

We spent the rest of the morning wandering and window-shopping and collecting a few things—accessories, mostly, ribbons and some junk jewelry.

As we headed back, one of the gallery windows caught my eye.

"Let's go in here," I said.

It was an art gallery, full of photographs. They were color photographs of people in distant lands. Obscure places like the Ukraine, the desert in Australia, jungles in Africa, Cambodia. Next to each photo was a printed sheet of paper with a story about the people in the picture. The photographer had traveled to these faraway lands, in the desert or the jungle or the ice, where small communities of people still lived, and stayed with them for weeks or even months and taken pictures. The landscapes were just as mesmerizing as the people.

I stared at one of an Aborigine family sitting on the porch of a dilapidated shack, somewhere in Australia. The father was holding an ax, the mother was mixing something in a large tin, and two little girls were in the front playing in the dirt. They were wearing tattered white dresses but looked happy. The landscape was flat and dry—I imagined they were in the desert with no neighbors for miles and miles and lived as best they could off the land. There was another photo of a community that lived in the wild jungles. Their houses were tucked into the mud and sat on high sticks.

Seeing all these photographs made me want to go to those places, talk to these people. I felt I knew them already. I wanted to take photos like this—photos that

137

captured people and places, together. Not just the environment, but people in their environment.

Melita tapped me on the shoulder and pointed to her
watch. "We've got to go meet Tomas," she said.

Twenty minutes later we sat on a park bench just inside
the square arches that led into Washington Square Park,
not saying anything. I kept looking through my camera at
various scenes. Little snippets of life: older kids hanging
out in groups and smoking, businesspeople walking by
talking on cell phones, homeless people wandering about.
Concrete and buildings and an occasional tree in the back-
ground were all part of what made the people and the
place one.

I put the camera down. Melita smiled at me and glanced
at her watch. "He should be here any minute."

As if on cue Tomas came running through the arches,
swinging his guitar case. He looked kind of classical in
cut-off khakis and a loose white T-shirt. He set the wide
end of the case down in front of us and rested his hands
on the neck. "I've got good news," he said. "I talked to
my uncle, and he said you can do the show this
Thursday."

"Oh my God!" Melita jumped off the bench and spun
around. An elegant dance move. "Hear that, Phoebe? We
can really do it! This is going to be a real event!"

My heart did a little flip of excitement. I hadn't thought
it would ever fall into place, that we would actually get
this far.

"And," Tomas continued, "Alex is in!"

"This is fabulous!" Melita threw her arms around
Tomas. "You're the best, you know that?"

The flip in my heart sank with the weight of jealousy. Whose idea was it in the first place? I was the one who knew the fairy tales. I was the one who had a trunk full of clothes. And I was the one who had brought them to New York. Why couldn't Melita and I just put on the show for ourselves?

"Let's hear you play," Melita said, still enthralled with Tomas's news.

Tomas took out his guitar and began tuning it. "This is just a warm-up," he explained. As he strummed, a couple of kids gathered around to listen. Tomas's notes began to form a folk tune, and he started to sing. It was a funny little song about wanting to be a fish and dancing on a star. With his accent, it sounded serious, even though it made no logical sense. You could tell Tomas really enjoyed playing the guitar. He closed his eyes, rocked his head back and forth to the music, and tapped his Doc Martens to the beat. When he finished, the kids applauded and asked for another song. Melita watched him as if she was one of the kids and he was her hero.

She inched closer to me and squeezed my hand. Her touch took me by surprise, and I jumped back. She just smiled as if to say, "See what we've done? See how far we've come?" I found her hand again, and with that simple touch I forgave her. Of course this was our show, but a show needs other people and an audience to work. It wasn't really a show with just the two of us, when we were making the outfits and talking about it. Now it was becoming real. It was coming alive.

"This one I thought might be suitable for Little Red Riding Hood," Tomas said. He started playing a piece that sounded classical. It started out light and airy, almost otherworldly, and then became dark and foreboding.

I took a picture of him as he played, his eyes closed, head back, fingers plucking the strings by heart. A small bead of sweat fell down his pointed nose. It looked like he was lost somewhere in the notes. I wondered where he went and if it was like anywhere I went sometimes when I watched things through my camera or read a story I was really absorbed in. The piece he was playing felt like it could be in a Grimm forest where anything was possible; even a little girl in a red cape happily trotting to Grandma's house could run into a menacing wolf. I don't know how Tomas found such a perfect piece to capture the mood, but he did.

Listening to him play and watching the people around me got me thinking. Maybe people are more than what we think they are, more than they appear on the surface. Sometimes Melita looks stuck up and smug, but she's deeper than that. Tomas looks like he has only one thing on his mind, but when he played the guitar I could just tell there was a lot of other stuff in there, too. Alex looks like a boy, and some people probably think she is, but she doesn't care. Michael looks like a farmer, but he is planning to go to college and study English literature. Gerelyn looks happy and self-assured, yet underneath that she's also sad and insecure. And my father? Did he look like a guy who had lost the one person he loved the most and had to raise two kids on a farm by himself? And then there's me. With my long hair I looked one way, and now with it short, I looked another. With my camera, did I look like a photographer? All the people I took photographs of, ones I knew and ones I didn't, have a story behind them. How they look barely skims the surface of that story. People, whether they live in New York City or in Plattville, Maine, all have something underneath them. Something they are not telling.

Melita acted as if she liked me *and* Tomas. Could she like us both? I didn't know. But as I watched Tomas play, I knew that the only way I could find out was to be brave and ask her. But it would have to be when the time was right. Which wasn't then.

When Tomas finished, Melita dropped my hand and applauded. "That's perfect," she said.

Tomas grinned a goofy grin and turned a bright shade of red. It was so obvious that he had a crush on Melita. He actually looked endearing with his mouth open and his eyes gaping. I felt a little sorry for him. I knew what it was like.

"Don't you think that's perfect, Phoebe?" Melita turned to me, waiting.

"Yah," I said. "It sounded good."

"It was just like *Red Riding Hood*," Melita said.

"I'm so glad you didn't want heavy metal or anything," Tomas said. "When you first said 'a fashion show,' I thought you might want runway kind of music, but this is much more suave."

Just then Alex showed up. "What's suave?" she asked.

Tomas strummed a few notes.

"That is suave. Very cool," Alex said. "So tell me about this show and what you want me to do. Tomas said it was very hip and feminist."

Melita explained how we got the idea and what we

141

planned to do. "And we need another person to do two of the characters. I'm doing three, but I can persuade Phoebe to do only one."

"I'm mostly the photographer," I said.

"Cool." Alex nodded, and I liked her immediately for not asking why. "Which one?"

"Rapunzel," I said and told her about my braids. "Plus I connect with Rapunzel. It feels as though I've been locked in a tower most of my life."

I don't know what made me say that. All three of them looked at me as if I was a little strange. But it was true, I *was* like Rapunzel. Except that I had cut my hair on purpose and I grew up around men. Well, Dad and Phil, if they count, and Michael.

"I'm doing Snow White, Sleeping Beauty, and Little Red Riding Hood. That leaves Cinderella and the Little Mermaid," Melita said.

"The Little Mermaid's not really a Grimm tale," I explained. "She's from Hans Christian Andersen. But she's sort of an icon, so we thought it was okay to include her."

"Plus she's got a way cool outfit. Fins and everything," Melita said.

"Topless?" Alex asked.

"Well, she should be, but to keep this PG we gave her some shells to wear."

Alex looked disappointed. I think she would have gone topless if she could have. I wondered what she thought she was going to show off. She made me look busty.

"Should we practice before we go on? At least I should know if I fit in the costumes."

"Yeah," Tomas said. "We've only got four days. Can we go to your place sometime and rehearse for real?"

I glanced at Melita. Would she bring Tomas back if Gerelyn was there? She gave me a quick nod and said, "Sure. How about tomorrow?"

19

Melita paced up and down in her bedroom, the late-morning sun streaming in and making her skin glow. She couldn't stop chattering.

"This is like our first date," she said. "Except you and Alex will be there, but that's how it starts. I don't know why I'm so nervous. What am I going to do all day? God, what am I going to wear?"

I sat on the lounge chair and watched her go through her closet, rejecting things in a heap on the bed. I knew how those discarded clothes felt.

"I've got to do something to calm down." She sat down on the floor and redid her ankle tattoo. Then she painted her toenails a dark red color with little flecks of gold in it. Then she painted mine. She kept talking. She told me about the four boys she had kissed. The first one was in second grade. "Billy Thrombone was his name. And he played the trombone. No kidding. I bet he gets teased for that name now. I wonder if he still plays. Then there was Patrick. He was sweet on me. I liked him, too. Then Alfanso, and then last year there was Peter."

"What happened to them all?" I asked.

"I moved. That's what happened. Plus I didn't want to

do certain things. I'm not ready to give all of myself to anyone yet. I can't be tied down. It's going to take someone special."

"Like Tomas?" I almost choked on the question.

"Maybe. Maybe not." She patted her nails to see if they were dry. "This isn't working," she said, jumping up.

"They look good," I said.

"Not the nails. Come on, I know the perfect distraction medicine."

Two subway rides later we found ourselves at Saks Fifth Avenue, the world-famous department store, in the cosmetics section behind a small pink partition, getting facials and makeovers. It was, of course, Melita's idea. "It'll be helpful to get tips for the show" was her reasoning. I just thought it might be fun, and why not? We needed a little relaxation and some air-conditioning.

"Lie back and relax," the cosmetic saleswoman said as she placed us side by side in padded swivel chairs. Her hand, with its long ruby nails, smeared my face with green mud.

"This is like algae from the pond," I said.

Melita snorted. "You'll have to forgive her," she said to the saleswoman. "She's from the country. Really out in the sticks. She does things like cut the tail off her sheep with a rubber band."

I felt my face redden underneath the green. The woman went on speaking in her high-pitched, energetic voice.

"Actually, all our products are natural and not tested on animals. Some of them even include ingredients similar to algae. Seaweed, for example, is an excellent exfoliator for problem and teenage skin."

I grinned at Melita.

Over the partition we could hear the other customers walk by and occasionally see the tops of their heads. It wasn't easy to relax with all the commotion going on, plus the mud on my face was beginning to dry and crack.

The woman came toward me—her orange-dyed, over-sprayed hair sticking straight up—and covered my face with a warm, wet cloth.

"This will dampen the mask and allow for ultimate results," she explained. We had gone to three counters before we found one that was able to do two facials without an appointment. This saleswoman was more than enthusiastic. I hoped she wouldn't be too disappointed when we didn't buy anything from her.

"You girls are smart to be here at your age. You're never too young to start taking proper care of your skin." I could hear Melita chuckling from the other chair, but the woman went on unfazed. "Young skin is so soft and supple. We're going to make you radiant. After we wash off the mud pack, your skin will emerge to its natural glow, free of all the outside debris that locks itself deep into the pores and accumulates dirt and oil. When it's properly cleaned and breathing freely, we'll cover it with a natural foundation to keep beauty and cleanliness in, grime and dirt out."

Was she for real? It was a good thing Melita and I were both hidden under cloth or we would have burst into hysterics.

I heard the water running and the clicking of her heels come closer. Her perfume was so overpowering, I had to hold my breath to keep from gagging.

She peeled the washcloth off, and her long, cool fingers massaged my cheeks. It felt nice. I closed my eyes so I wouldn't have to look into her pancaked face and eyes, which were stretched out to her ears with eyeliner. She was probably all freckles underneath, but you'd never know it for all the powder she had on. Her bright pink lips were outlined with an even brighter pink. Everyone and everything seemed exaggerated in New York. This woman was promoting all these natural products, yet she was the most unnatural person I'd ever seen. And all she was doing was trying to fit in.

"Now a bit of toner," she said when she had finished massaging and had removed the algae. I opened my eyes, and she gleamed down at me with a cotton ball in her hand. Her teeth were exceptionally white and large.

"This is a cucumber-lemon toner to tighten and freshen." She described each product and explained what it did. They were all supposed to do more or less the same thing—cleanse, freshen, tighten. She talked nonstop, and when she ran out of things to say, she hummed, running back and forth between the two of us.

The cleansing routine was complete, and now it was time for our light makeup application. "Now with young faces like yours we don't want to overdo it. The trick to applying makeup is to accentuate your best features. We'll start with you, Melita."

Melita sat up. This woman was completely serious, and Melita played right along as if it were a game. How far we were from that day by the pond, I thought. That seemed like years ago. And now I was in New York City, getting a facial.

"I'm worried about my nose," Melita said. "You see how it tilts to one side. Isn't there anything I can do to make it look straighter?"

"You have an exceptional face. One thing you'll notice about models is that they all have a feature that makes them unique. Your nose is yours. I bet all the boys are after you in school."

Melita shrugged. That was one of the good things about Melita; people could rave on and on about her looks, but she couldn't care less.

"Let's focus on your beautiful eyes and full lips, and your skin is so supple and smooth." She went on complimenting Melita's features. I wondered what on earth she would find to compliment on me.

When she finished, Melita really did look good. Not overdone like the woman.

"Okay, now for you," the saleswoman said to me.

"Phoebe," I offered, in case she'd forgotten my name.

"Yes. Phoebe. A lovely name."

Great. My best feature was my name.

"You have beautiful coloring, Phoebe. What I wouldn't give for a natural red like yours." She put her hand to her own fiery orange, sprayed mass.

"I got it cut this summer. It used to be down to here." I pointed to my waist. "But I always had to wear it in braids or it got tangled something fierce."

"It's a good cut for you."

I could practically feel Melita beaming, but to my surprise she didn't say anything.

The saleswoman moved to my eyes. "Exquisite," she said. "Such an unusual green. But your lashes are so light and thin! You could benefit from a lash tint. Then you never have to worry about mascara. We do them here and it lasts about six weeks."

"Not today," I said. Eyelash tinting! I'd never heard of such a thing. I imagined telling my father I'd had my lashes tinted. "Are you crazy? Your eyelashes are perfect the way they are," he'd say. "What do you need that artificial garbage for?" Dad won't even let me get my ears pierced because, he claims, it is unnatural.

She finished my makeup and turned me to the mirror. "There, what do you think?"

I hadn't transformed into a ravishing beauty, but I looked okay. I felt I was not quite the real me, but not quite someone else, either.

"Now what would you girls like to purchase this afternoon?"

I figured I'd let Melita handle this one. It was her idea to pretend that we were paying customers to get free facials. But she said, "I'll take some of the almond cleanser, the cucumber toner, the passion fruit lipstick, and midnight blue eyeliner."

"Excellent. And you?" she hummed to me.

"Nothing, thanks."

"She'll take the same. Oh, and mascara, too." She handed the woman a credit card. When the woman went to get the cosmetics, I nudged Melita.

"Relax," she whispered. "It's on Mom. She said I could use it to buy myself something. It's her way of not feeling guilty for getting you a camera."

The woman came back carrying a paper bag with rope handles. She thanked us and gave us her business card.

"Come back and see me when you need more. And remember, free and natural," she sang through her collagen-enhanced lips.

When we got outside, we were finally able to let loose.

"What a hoot. Could you believe her?" Melita stood on her tiptoes and imitated her, poofing up a make-believe ponytail. "Now remember, beauty and cleanliness in, grime and dirt out," she mimicked.

"This is to tighten, freshen, and uplift your glowing, young, radiant skin," I said, dabbing Melita's cheeks with my fingertips. We went on a bit, speaking in her funny, high voice.

"Give me your camera," she said, suddenly serious.

I handed it to her, knowing it was stupid to do so.

"I want to take *your* picture for once," she said.

"Oh, I don't know," I stammered.

"Come on. Stand there by the parking meter. I'll get you with some New York City cabs behind you. You can show your father and Phil to prove you were here."

"They know I'm here," I said but leaned against the meter anyway.

"Do something funny," Melita commanded.

I stood there, awkwardly swinging my arms while Melita snapped away.

"That's not funny," she said.

I made an attempt to show my teeth in an exaggerated grin and stuck out my tongue.

"Good." Melita clicked the picture. "Now look longing."

I drooped my eyes and pouted.

"Excellent. Now just look your natural self."

"Okay, okay. Enough," I said, reaching for the camera. But before I could get it, she put her face next to mine and held the camera out at arm's length. She snapped a picture and then gave the camera back. "Not bad for someone who likes to live behind the camera. But you still need to loosen up, Phoebe." She squeezed my shoulders and took my hand.

We walked through the park like that. I thought the heat would melt our makeup, but miraculously it lasted. I also thought I would want to wash it off immediately, but I was enjoying the feeling of being slightly different. It made me feel bold and daring and somewhat mischievous. I was pleased, too, that Melita seemed to be back to her normal self and that all afternoon she hadn't once mentioned Tomas.

20

On the way back, we stopped at a Japanese restaurant to get some sushi for dinner. Melita picked up some daisies from the vendor on her street corner. At the apartment, we set the table with tiny square dishes and chopsticks.

"Mom's at rehearsal all evening, so we won't be bothered," Melita said, arranging the flowers in a vase. She had decided to wear something casual after all, and had chosen a white, see-through blouse with a bright blue tank top underneath and cut-offs. I felt like we were getting ready for a dinner party. I wished I could have been more excited. I loved doing all the preparations with Melita, but then I dreaded the reason we were doing it. If only we could prep forever and never have to get to the actual event.

The door buzzed and made me jump. It was Alex. "Cool place," she said before she even got all the way through the door. She went over to Gerelyn's painting. "Wild."

Tomas came soon after. "You can't have sushi without sake," he said, holding up a bottle of wine. *Uh-oh*, I thought. *This can't lead to anything good.*

"Perfect," Melita said. "Mom's even got sake cups."

She brought back four small ceramic cups from the kitchen and set them next to the plates.

We arranged the sushi on the little plates, and Melita poured the warm wine into the little cups. Everything about Japanese food was small. I'd never eaten raw fish before, but I found if I closed my eyes and just plopped it in my mouth, I could hardly taste it.

"To the Grimm Brothers." Melita raised her glass.

"To the Grimm Sisters," Alex said.

"Hear, hear." Tomas clinked his glass with the others.

I raised my glass but didn't say anything. The sake tasted strong and bitter. It left a warm feeling on my tongue and in the back of my throat.

After dinner, Melita brought out the costumes, holding each one to her chest before draping it over the couch.

"Here's Cinderella." She handed Alex the gold burlap we had made into a dress.

Alex frowned for a second, then said, "Oh, I get it. You want her to look sexy without having to wear a fancy dress. But what about shoes? Do you have a glass slipper?"

"We thought she'd wear boots instead. Something that won't fall off her feet." Melita showed her the clear rubber boots we'd found in SoHo. "Neither of us can fit in these," she said.

"Just like Cinderella," Tomas laughed. "If they fit you, Alex, you will be the true princess, and I guess I will have to marry you."

Alex snorted. "Don't think you're my type, Tomas. Sorry." She pulled the boots on. You could see her bare feet through them, toe rings and all. She walked to the window and back. "A little loose, but I can walk fine. I'll have to wash my feet for Thursday."

"Maybe not. Maybe it'd be better to have a Cinderella with dirty feet. What do you think, Phoebe?" It was nice how Melita kept trying to draw me into the conversation, but I still felt like the third, or fourth, wheel.

"There's nothing wrong with dirty feet," I said.

We showed them the rest of the outfits. Or, rather, Melita showed and I nodded when she asked me something. I think the wine was making me very tired. It was all I could do to suppress my yawns. As soon as Tomas pulled out his guitar and started playing, I could barely keep my eyes open. But when it was my turn to practice being Rapunzel, I dutifully walked from the couch to the window and said the lines we'd come up with for her. Not only did each character walk in her outfit, but she also said something as that character.

"This is going to be such a blast," Melita said, clapping her hands when we were done.

"What now?" Tomas asked. He had been sitting next to Melita on the couch and moved closer to her. He put his hand on her knee.

"Anyone want to go out?" Melita asked.

"I can't," Alex said. "I've got to get going. But I'll see you all on Thursday, if not before." She bade us goodbye and left. I listened to her heavy footsteps clomp down the stairs. I was sorry to see her go. Somehow having Alex there took away from my having to be so aware of Melita and Tomas.

"Phoebe? What do you want to do? What more of New York do you want to see?" Melita asked.

I want to see you without Tomas, I thought. *To be back on the farm with just you.* The triplets were probably walking straight already, even Noodles. Suddenly I was exhausted. I should have been all excited to be in such a great big famous city with two tour guides, but all I wanted to do was to take a nap in a grassy field, rest my head on Melita's belly, and watch the clouds. Even being back at Saks getting facials would be better. Anything, anywhere, with Melita the way she was before Tomas.

"We could all go dancing," Tomas suggested.

"Dancing." Melita twirled around us both. Her body moved with ease, arms stretching up like a ballet dancer and hips shaking like a belly dancer. "Do you want to dance, Phoebe?" she asked, lifting me up from the couch. I started to feel dizzy and sat back down. Then she pulled Tomas up, and they danced together, her arms on his shoulders.

"Come on, Phoebe." Melita grabbed me again and held on to my elbow. Tomas took my other arm, and the three of us swayed together in a circle. Melita started to rub her hand down my arm. I shook her off and sat down again.

"I'll just stay here," I said.

"Are you sure?" Melita looked at me from behind Tomas. "When do you get to go dancing in Manhattan, country girl?"

"I'm pretty tired," I said, ignoring the country girl comment. "You guys go."

"Well, okay, if you're sure you don't mind."

"I don't mind," I said.

"You're the greatest, sweetie. Sweetie-Phoebe." She mouthed me a kiss. "Isn't she the greatest, Tomas?"

Tomas grinned and nodded.

"That's why you're my best friend." Melita came over and kissed my cheek. "I'll just be a second. I want to change," she said to Tomas. She ran into the bedroom, leaving me and Tomas staring at each other in an awkward silence.

"Do you like Melita?" I finally got the nerve to ask.

"Oh, yes, sure. She is great."

I nodded.

"She is a lot of fun," he added.

I nodded again. *But do you know anything about her? I wanted to ask. Do you know how she's moved a zillion times? Do you know about her mother? Do you know she has no close friends except for me? Do you know that we've kissed?* Of course I didn't ask any of this.

"Do you?" he asked.

"What?" I asked.

"Do you like Melita?"

I wasn't sure what he meant by "like." It was so much easier for me to ask that question than to answer it. Yes, I did like Melita. A lot. I found her fun, too. But also mysterious and exciting and beautiful.

"Of course," I said.

"You and she are so different," he said. "It's funny that you are friends."

Yah, well, you're funny, too, I thought, *with your accent and your ponytail and your eyes-closed guitar playing. And not in the ha-ha way.*

I didn't say anything else, and finally Melita came back, wearing a brown suede minidress and striped leggings.

"Thanks so much for being understanding," she

whispered to me. "I owe you one." She hugged me tight and gave me a peck on the nose. "Don't wait up," she said, tugging Tomas to the door.

I watched out the window as they crossed the street and headed up the block, then disappeared around the corner. I looked around the apartment, not sure what to do now that I was alone. I'd taken only a couple of sips of wine, so I didn't think I was drunk, but maybe just a little bit tipsy. I put the rest of the sake away and cleaned up the kitchen. Then I put some music on the CD player and sat on the couch. Gerelyn's painting loomed over me. It glowed under the lights, so I switched them off. I lay on the couch thinking of home, thinking of the softness of Melita, of Melita with Tomas. My head was throbbing and my face felt hot. I closed my eyes. I wanted to know if Melita thought of me in the same way, if our kiss had meant anything to her. But I was also afraid to know. I was stuck in limbo.

I reached for the phone, pulled Michael's number from my pocket, and dialed.

"Hello?" a woman's voice answered.

"This is Phoebe," I said, clearing my throat. "Michael gave me this number."

"Oh, Phoebe! Michael's told me so much about you. I'm Kate, his sister. He says you're like a little sister to him."

"Is he there?" I asked.

"Hold on. I hope I get to meet you someday."

"Me, too," I said.

"Phoebe? Is everything okay?" Michael's voice was rushed. Did that happen to everyone in the city? Everybody seemed to be in a bigger rush than the next person, except for the homeless people, who merely sat silently in one place, never moving anything but their eyes.

"I . . . uh . . ." I started. "Yah, everything's okay, I guess." Suddenly I wasn't sure why I'd called.

"Where are you?" he asked.

"At Gerelyn's. Melita went out with a friend."

"And didn't take you? That's kind of rude."

"No," I said quickly. "She asked me. I didn't want to go."

"Oh, well what's up, then?"

"I just wanted to hear a familiar voice," I said.

"Yah, I know how that is. Don't you feel a long way from home? I sure do."

I smiled. Maybe he was homesick, too. "Manhattan is nothing like Plattville," I said.

"That's for sure." Michael laughed his sturdy deep laugh. "Just think of all the stories you'll have when you get home."

"And pictures," I said, thinking of all the rolls of film I'd already shot.

"Have you called your father yet?"

"Yes, Michael," I said, rolling my eyes even though he couldn't see. "I called him the night I got here."

"So what have you been doing this week?" he asked.

I told him about going to Broadway and Saks Fifth Avenue, Saint Mark's Place, the gallery, and about Gerelyn buying me a camera. "And we've been hanging out in this café," I said, "where Melita has some friends." I couldn't quite bring myself to tell him about Tomas. The thought of actually saying it out loud made it seem so petty and insignificant.

"That sounds very New York," Michael said.

"We're going to do that fashion show there."

"That's great! Can I come?"

"Sure," I said, thinking how nice it would be if he were there.

"I wouldn't want to miss it," he said. "And I'm sure Kate will want to come, too."

I told him where and when.

"I've got to go now, Phoeb. We're getting on the subway, and I don't think these things work underground. You take care now, okay?"

"Okay," I said. "Thanks, Michael." I hung up and flopped back on the couch.

I woke up to the sound of the door being unlocked. *Robbers,* I thought, and instinctively jumped behind the couch to hide.

"Shhh," someone whispered. There was a giggle as someone backed into the hall table. Melita. And Tomas.

Before I knew it, Melita had walked over to the couch and turned on the lamp. I crouched as low as I could on the floor. They couldn't see me.

"Come here, you," she said, plopping herself down and patting the couch pillows. My heart thumped.

Tomas sat next to her, and I saw his arm go around her shoulder and gently massage it.

"Mmm. That feels nice." Melita snuggled against him.

"No one is here?" he asked.

"Mom must be out still, and Phoebe is probably sleeping. Don't wake her."

"No, let's not wake her."

159

Melita giggled foolishly.

I hated Tomas at that moment more than anything.

"Oh, come on, Phoebe's my friend," Melita said.

"I think your friend has a little crush on you."

"Phoebe? She's just excited because she has a friend. She doesn't get out much on that farm she lives on. I've been there. It's really in the sticks. Phoebe hides behind that camera of hers. She lives in a fantasy world and thinks someday she'll find her prince charming. She's so naive."

"Don't talk anymore," Tomas said. I saw his hands go around Melita's neck and his long, thick, oh-so-beautiful hair drape over the couch as they kissed.

I tried to shrink myself against the couch. Everything was quiet. New York City must never have been so quiet. Not a car driving by, not a person yelling in the street, not even a cat howling. Nothing except the sound of Melita and Tomas kissing. I held my breath, but the tears came anyway. And I hiccupped at the exact moment in which Tomas opened his eyes and stared down at me.

21

I bolted. I somehow undid all those locks, ran down three flights of stairs, out the front door, and into the dark street. I heard Melita calling after me, but I kept running and didn't look back. I could've turned around and told her that I was jealous of Tomas, that I wanted her all for myself. But how could anyone say that stuff? Would she understand? How could she, when *I* didn't even understand? And what she'd said to Tomas sounded like I was nothing to her.

I ran to the park, figuring I'd just sit for a few minutes until I knew what to do. The sky had a hazy, nighttime glow, but it must have been earlier than I thought, since plenty of people were still wandering about. I focused on the scenes around me, separating them from each other and the rest of the park. I spied a man and a woman wrapped in each other's arms on a bench. Two men holding hands walked by. There seemed to be loving and kissing in all forms. Men with men, women with women, men with women.

Without my camera I felt bare, exposed. Melita was right—I did hide behind that stupid lens and my fairy tale ideas. I thought everyone would stop and stare at me, point and laugh, or ask me what I was doing out there all alone. But they were absorbed in their own lives. No one noticed me—one lone girl sitting on a bench looking at the world.

I could find the bus station, get a ticket home. Except I had no money on me. I'd left my wallet at Melita's. I didn't even have any change to call Michael and ask him to come and rescue me. I thought about begging for some. I even stuck my cupped palm out. All I had to say was, "Please, can you spare some change? I'm trying to get home." It struck me that maybe that's all the homeless are trying to do—get themselves home. I put my hand down.

It was dark. I knew I couldn't stay in the park. Some shady-looking characters were already lurking about. I'd have to go back. I'd have to face Melita sooner or later. She probably hated me now, or thought I was some silly immature kid, too selfish to be happy for her. And maybe I was.

A guy drinking from a bottle wrapped in a paper bag walked by. "Smile, it's a beautiful night," he said.

I nodded, gave a small smile, but got up quickly and headed back to Melita's, my hands in my pockets, my head low, and my heart broken. *This isn't supposed to be how it ends,* I thought. It's not even supposed to begin this way. It begins with a princess and ends with a prince. Even the scariest fairy tales end with a happy marriage. Even in *Bluebeard,* where the woman discovers she has married a murderer, she ends up destroying him and marrying a noble and honest man.

I looked up. No stars. Just lights and buildings and, in between, a strip of night sky. But it was the same sky as on the farm, and it was beautiful in its own way. I circled around with my neck bent back, staring at all the views.

Right then, I knew I'd never end up being rescued by a prince. Not Michael, not anyone closer to my age. I'd never be rescued by a princess, either. So I figured I'd just have to buck up and rescue myself.

I swung my arms and held my head high as I made this resolution. I arrived at Melita's door. I'd have to ring the buzzer to be let in. Who knew if Melita was still there? And Tomas? Melita had chased me down the stairs, but I had lost her once I got outside. Maybe they were happy I was gone. Maybe they were having sex. I could see Tomas grinning away as he pawed Melita. Humping like goats. An image of Petunia with a buck came to mind, but I quickly shook it away. I raised my arm to press the buzzer just as a taxi pulled up and a long arm stretched out the window.

Gerelyn called to me. "Phoebe? Is that you? Wait up. I'll let you in."

I watched her get out of the car. Elegant, graceful, crazy—Gerelyn.

She rushed up, fumbling with her keys. "You're out late, hon. Where's Mel?"

"She's inside. I had to get some air."

Gerelyn looked me in the eye. "Everything okay, honey?" She smiled a big warm smile. At that moment I may have despised Melita for betraying me, but I loved her mother and forgave her everything she'd ever done to Melita. It wasn't her fault. She loved her daughter, anyone could see that. And she was trying. That's all anyone could ask of a mother. Of anyone.

I threw my arms around her. I couldn't help it. And I burst into loud, heaving sobs.

"Oh, honey pie. There, there." She opened the front door, and we shuffled inside. And right there in the foyer, we hugged. She didn't even pry or ask me what was wrong. Just patted me and said over and over, "There, there. Let it out. Let it out."

I cried for a good long while. Finally I began to slow down, and I moved my head away from her shoulder. She gave me a tissue and I blew my nose. There was slobber all over her dress. "Sorry," I mumbled.

"Not a problem. Nothing a little soap and water can't get out," she said.

"I don't know what came over me. I didn't mean to blubber all over you like that." I wiped my face.

"It's okay. I've certainly done my share of blubbering. It can be good to have a good blubber every so often. Makes you see things fresh."

"Really?" I said. "But I'm so confused."

"We are all confused," Gerelyn said. "Life is like that. Just when we think we have it all figured out—whammo!—it goes and confuses us. It's how we deal with it that matters." She patted me on the back. "You've had a lot to deal with. And your father, bless his heart, shelters you because he loves you so much. It must be hard for you to sort things out with no mother around."

Hard for *me*? *I* had a lot to deal with? Until recently it didn't seem like I had anything to deal with. Sure, I missed not having a mom to talk to sometimes, but I never even knew her. And that's just life, isn't it?

"Do you want to talk, sweetheart?" Gerelyn asked. And that sent me crying all over again. I did want to talk, but about what? How could I ever say everything? About not knowing what my mother was like? About not having any friends before Melita? About what I felt inside?

I took a breath and asked, "What do you do if you think you love someone, but you don't know if they love you? Well, you know they probably love you, but not in the same way?"

Gerelyn nodded and murmured, "Mmmm. Unrequited love." She mulled my question over for a moment, then said, "What you do is tell them how you feel. If they love you at all, it will be okay."

"And if they don't?" I asked.

"Then you'll be okay. You're a very strong and capable young woman, Phoebe. You are so much like your mother that way."

"I wish I could have known my mother," I said. "I wish she had never died. I wish that my father understood me more."

"Your father does what he thinks is best. He does it out of love. And he might understand more than you think he does. You should try him. But you know, you can still call me anytime, Phoebe, if you want to talk about female stuff. I may not have been the best mom all the time to Melita, but I am recovering now, and I have a lot to make up for. I could use two daughters to help teach me. Your mother taught me a lot, and I'd be honored to know her daughter."

I was proud to be my mother's daughter all of a sudden.

Gerelyn wanted to know me because of who my mom was and because I was a strong young woman. "Thank you," I said. I stood straighter.

"Shall we go upstairs now? See Melita? Have a cup of tea?" Gerelyn asked.

"I think Melita might be mad at me," I said.

"All the more reason to see her." We walked up the stairs in silence. I felt like I was walking into the unknown. What would be waiting for me? Would I enter as a different person?

The second I opened the door, Melita ran over, phone in hand, and started screaming. "Oh my God! Where did you go? We were freaking out! I was about to call the police. Do you know there are muggers and rapists out there at night? And you don't even know the city!" She embraced me tightly. "Don't ever do that again. I was so worried."

"Looks like she's real mad," Gerelyn said.

I stepped back from Melita and glanced around. "Where's Tomas?" I asked.

"I told him to go look for you. I decided to wait here in case you came back. Which you did, thank God." The phone rang. "That must be him."

She answered it and paused a second before saying, "She's here. Just came in with Mom. She looks fine."

I had my eyes on the floor so I couldn't see Melita's face, but I saw her twist one leg behind the other.

"Thanks, Tomas. Yeah, I had fun, too. I'm glad she's back, too. I'll tell her." She hung up and said to us, "He's going home now. And he wanted to apologize to you, Phoebe."

"Tomas was here and I didn't get to meet him?" Gerelyn said. "Apologize for what?"

"It's nothing, really, Mom. Just a misunderstanding. Maybe you'll get to meet him some other time."

For the first time since I went in, I dared to look Melita in the eye.

"I'm not sure if he's going to be my boyfriend or not, but I like hanging out with him," she said. I wasn't sure if this was for my benefit or Gerelyn's.

"Well, there's no rush, Mel. You have your whole life to make good choices." Gerelyn put her hand on Melita's cheek.

Melita rolled her eyes. "Mom. Anyway, you can meet him at the show. That is, if you can come."

"Of course I can come, sweetie. I wouldn't miss it for the world. I'll skip rehearsal if I have to." She kissed Melita. "I'm going to put the kettle on. You girls look like you could use some tea. It's been quite an evening."

When the tea was brewed and Gerelyn had gone to bed, Melita and I sat in the kitchen. At first we just looked at each other. Then we both started to say "I'm sorry" at the same time. Then we burst into laughter and hugged. The laughter turned to tears, then laughter, then tears again, and so on, until neither of us could muster any more emotion and we broke apart.

Melita said, "I can't believe I said those things about you. I didn't mean them. I just said them. I thought it would impress Tomas."

I still wasn't sure what to believe.

"Tomas wants you," I said.

"Yeah, well, I don't know if I want him. He's nice and

handsome and all, but I think he wants to move a little too fast for me. I don't think I need a boyfriend right now. I need a friend."

My pulse raced a little at this news. I was her friend. She needed me.

"You can have any guy you want, Melita. You're so beautiful."

"Oh, Phoebe. You're just saying that. I'm not really."

"Melita, you are beautiful. How can you not know that?"

"Sure, maybe as a baby I was. And what does that matter? Look at me now. I can't keep friends. I meet people but no one who really cares. And when I finally make one true friend, I go and blow it by being a jerk. And my nose is crooked!"

"I care," I said. "You haven't blown it with me. And I think your nose is perfect."

She smiled through her tears. "I'm not like you, Phoebe. You're smart and you have something you love. You have a passion. All I really know how to do is buy nice things and put on makeup."

"That is so not true. You are the most amazing person I have ever met. You have so much energy. Everything sparkles and comes alive when you're around."

"Really?"

"Really. I cannot even believe I am giving *you* this pep talk. You're the one who's always making *me* feel beautiful."

Melita wiped her nose. "I'm not as secure as you think, Phoebe. I'm not perfect."

We were silent for a minute. No, I guess Melita was not perfect. Perhaps no one is.

"You are cute," she said, touching my shoulder. "And I mean cute in a beautiful way. Someone great is going to really fall for you someday."

I blushed and we hugged—a nice long, close hug. And I knew in my heart that that someone was not going to be her. She started rubbing her hands up my back. I took a deep breath and pulled away.

"Melita," I said. "I have to tell you something. Something important."

"Okay," she said.

"It might change things, but I have to tell you because you are my best friend."

"What? What is it?"

"When we kissed, it really meant something to me." I took another deep breath and went on. "Every time we touch it means something. I think I love you. Really love you. You might be grossed out or hate me, but it's true."

My heart was racing, but it felt good to say that out loud. A tremendous relief. But then I held my breath again as Melita processed it.

She sat there, watching the street below.

"Say something," I said, pleading.

She turned to me and sighed. *Here it comes*, I thought, not knowing exactly what "it" was.

"There's so much I don't know. I think I like Tomas, but then I'm not sure. I don't hate you. I love you, too. But I just don't know if it's the same way. I'm confused." She sat back and breathed. Maybe this was hard for her, too.

"It's okay to be confused," I said, quoting Gerelyn.

"I don't know," she said. "Is it okay to love you but not know how? Or not understand it?"

"It's okay," I said. I sounded so sure. Maybe I was. "Life is confusing. People are complicated."

"I mean, is it okay for you? Can you still be friends with me?"

"Oh." I thought for a second. "I think so. I want to be friends."

Melita wiped away a tear. "Me, too," she said. "I mean, I want to be friends with you." We both laughed and hugged again.

22

Thursday came, and we did the show.

Michael was in the audience with his sister, who had curly hair and a friendly smile, just like him. Gerelyn sat behind him with a friend of hers from the play—a long, lanky man with a goatee. (A date?) Some of Tomas's and Alex's friends were there and a couple of people Melita had invited from her school. Tomas's uncle stood by the coffee bar, keeping things running. And a number of café customers just wandered by out of curiosity. There was a basket by the door with a tag that read "Donations" in large red letters.

Tomas was onstage, perched on a stool, strumming a tune on his guitar and looking appropriately dreamy. I milled about with my camera.

Melita and Alex were in the bathroom. I sneaked in and joined them.

"How does it look out there?" Melita asked.

"There's a crowd," I said. "All the seats we moved are taken."

"Yikes. I didn't think I'd be nervous, but I am. Can you help me with this zipper?" Melita turned her back to me, and I zipped up her Sleeping Beauty dress.

"You'll do great," I said.

Melita flashed me her smile, the one that crinkled her eyes and dimpled her cheeks. "I know," she said. "Thanks." She squeezed me tight.

"Break a leg, Melita," Alex said.

"You, too," she said.

I went out first and stood to the side of the stage. I nodded to Tomas's uncle, who lowered the lights. Tomas started his *Sleeping Beauty* tune, and Melita walked out of the bathroom in her flowing dress with all the layers of gauze. She stepped dramatically up the three steps to the stage and sashayed across the platform. She slowly walked to the center and said in a bellowing voice, "I am Sleeping Beauty. I have slept for one hundred years. I was so sick and tired of the world and its oppression that I wanted to tune it all out, to wait until it was worth waking up and I was ready to participate. When I finally woke, it was the future and I was here. I am awake now. I am very well rested and there's no stopping me!" She walked to the edge of the stage in slow motion. The inner folds of her dress caressed her body, and the outer folds fluttered like butterflies all around her as she turned around one more time. I clicked the camera throughout, shooting as fast as I could.

When I put it down for a second, Melita caught my eye and winked. Her eyes were made up with silver eye shadow that glistened in the light. Even her hair had sparkles in it, making the red stripe glow against her natural black. She was in her element. I turned to look at Gerelyn, who was absolutely beaming with pride. The audience clapped as Melita disappeared through the bathroom door.

Alex was next, as Cinderella. She wore the gold burlap sack. We had gathered it slightly in front with a shimmery ribbon, so it looked more like a minidress. She wore the clear rubber boots and had painted her toenails blood red. She stomped to center stage. Tomas played something wilder, a rockabilly tune.

Alex cleared her throat and said, "I am Cinderella. I go from working at home to going out on the town with no problem. I left the prince soon after we met. He only wanted me to wear dainty, uncomfortable high heels and still expected me to clean up after him." She lifted her foot and stomped it down heavily for effect. The audience applauded and someone whistled. "But I like being in the dirt, and now I have a gardening business and date whomever I please."

I snapped pictures of her as she walked off.

Melita came out again, this time as Little Red Riding Hood. We had worked so hard on this outfit, getting the dog costume to look like a wolf. When we were sewing it, I felt like the woman in *Rumpelstiltskin* weaving straw into gold until her fingers bled. But it looked more like a wolf cape now than a dog one, draped over Melita's shoulders and tied around her neck. The red pleather pants reflected the light as she walked. Her black hair was tucked under a red beret, and her boots were shiny, black, and high-heeled. "I am Red Riding Hood. I'm not so little and I'm not so naive. I killed that wolf and saved Granny. We will be eating fresh meat all year," she said and opened the cape even more to expose the knife case around her waist. The crowd cheered, and someone even hollered out, "That's right, sister!"

173

Red Riding Hood did her turn across the stage and exited.

Then Alex came back as the Little Mermaid. She scuffed across the stage in her fish legs. I didn't get to hear her speech, though, since I had to go change into my Rapunzel outfit. I handed the camera to Michael before I went into the bathroom. He said he'd take pictures for me. Melita insisted that we have the whole show documented, though I'd have been happy to leave my part out of it.

The bathroom light seemed extra bright after the dimness of the café. The sink was littered with makeup, and outfits were strewn about willy-nilly.

"It's going well, don't you think?" Melita brought me the green velvet Rapunzel dress. It was a sleeveless top with a short, flared skirt. Underneath I wore tight black running shorts. We figured Rapunzel would have to move with ease. I slipped on the dress.

"You look great out there," I said. "Alex, too. I think people are really getting into it."

"Are you ready?" Melita asked.

I nodded. She removed my braid from its plastic bag and attached it to my scalp with at least a hundred bobby pins. Having my hair back made my head feel heavy. I had forgotten what it was like to carry around this extra weight. The one long braid fell past my butt.

"The fairy tales have come to life," Melita said. "And they are us."

"Very profound," I said jokingly. But maybe there was a little truth to it. It was as though we'd created our own fairy tale just by putting this show together from beginning to end.

"Break a leg," Alex said as she entered the bathroom. "It's your turn, girl."

Melita gave me a gentle shove toward the door.

And there I was, with barely a moment to think or to get terrified, walking up the steps. I didn't even trip. The café seemed really still and Tomas's guitar twanged in the darkness. Everyone was staring at me. Me. Phoebe Sharp from Plattville, Maine, acting as Rapunzel.

I saw Michael. He gave me a wave and a thumbs-up before he took a picture of me. His sister smiled. Tomas nodded as I passed by him and kept playing. The tune he had for me was a melodramatic, choppy number, like the sound of someone jumping over rocks. I got to the center and did my spin around, then held the microphone in both hands. They were shaking. I caught Gerelyn's face grinning up at me encouragingly. I took a deep breath, then spoke.

"Hello." My voice didn't sound like mine when magnified by the mike. It made it easier to talk. "I am Rapunzel. I was locked in a tower, but I am light as a feather and can float away on my dreams and my imagination whenever I desire. I have learned to scale walls and can fly through the forest. I let down my hair whenever I can. I am not tied by extra weight." I took the bobby pins out and released my braid. I lifted it over my head and waved it like a lasso. "I have never been more free!" I shouted. My heart was beating wildly, and I was sure everyone could hear it. Then the audience started clapping and drowned it out, until all I could hear was applause ringing in my ears, and throughout my body I could feel the sound of hands clapping. I took a bow and walked off the stage, passing Melita in her final outfit as I entered the bathroom. The bathroom door closed behind me and everything became quiet, except for my heart still beating like a drum. I looked at myself in the mirror. *I did it,* I thought. And that was that.

Alex and I stood in the doorway as Melita did her final turn as Snow White. She made a great Snow White, dressed in a white silk dress, with a slit up to her thigh. She wore a red heart clip in her hair. When she came down the stairs, the three of us joined hands and walked back up together. We raised our arms and said in unison, just like we had practiced, "We are free! We are here!" We all bowed together.

And then it was over. Applause and some cheers. Afterward everyone milled around like a real reception, drinking lattes and eating carrot cake and telling us how great we were, how imaginative and creative, how professional and fun. Gerelyn said my mother would have been proud. Michael gave me his second kiss on the cheek. Our show was over, and my time in New York was winding down. I was ready to go home.

Country

23

I headed down the path by the barn with a pailful of blackberries and scratches all over my arms. I had forgotten to wear long sleeves, as usual. This always happens when I go berrying. I can't help getting all cut up. I guess it's part of the thrill. I always see the biggest, juiciest berry deep in the thicket of briars, and that's the one I have to get. Blackberries were my favorite, but they also meant summer was close to its end.

"Hi, Petunia," I said, stopping by the fence. She came running over, the triplets close behind. I held out some berries in my palm. The triplets greedily gobbled them down and then nibbled my fingers. They were all walking steadily now, even Noodles. I decided I would still call her that. It suited her.

"Easy, girls. I've got to bring some back or these scratches won't have been worth it."

I went over to the pond. The bark on the willow tree glistened in the sunlight, and the branch over the water cast a deep shadow. The leaves were already fading pale yellow. The sky was a swirling mix of blue and white, and the breeze across the algae made a rippling of greens. Such colors. One of the roosters crowed in the distance. I stood by my mother's grave. Carol Olsen Sharp. I chose three of the best blackberries and placed them on the ground by her stone, then walked back toward the house.

Dad came by with a bucket of mulch for the garden. "There you are," he said. He stared at my arms. "Oh, Phoebe, you didn't go berrying without covering up again, did you?"

I stretched out my arms. Some of the scratches had already welted up. "It doesn't hurt," I said.

"You'd better go and put some lotion on. It'll take some of the redness away."

"But it was worth it. Look." I held up the can of berries. "I got the biggest ones."

"I'll bet. Probably the highest, too." He took a couple and popped them in his mouth. "They are delicious. But next time cover up, okay?"

"Sure." I grinned.

He headed off, then turned. "Oh, you got a phone call."

"Melita?" I asked. We'd been calling each other every couple of days since I got back and e-mailing every day. We talked about everything. Gerelyn's play was opening in a week, and Melita had been going to some of the rehearsals. There might even be a small part for her mom in another play. I might be able to go back to New York over the winter vacation to see it.

"A girl named Beth," Dad said. "I wrote her number by the phone."

I hadn't exactly forgotten about Beth and the newspaper, but I also hadn't expected her to call. Ever since I had run into her at Tiny's, I had thought about why she was so nice to me. Maybe she remembered when we used to play together, too.

I rinsed the berries in the kitchen sink, then went to my room and rubbed lotion on my forearms and legs. I took my time and covered all the scratches.

I stretched out on my bed. I untucked my T-shirt and pulled it up to my neck, exposing my bare chest. I cupped one of my breasts. A handful of breast. I cupped the other one. Two little mounds of flesh. They fit snugly in my hands. It seemed they hadn't been so snug a few months ago. I know I'll never be buxom like Gerelyn, but maybe there was hope after all. In the spring I had bought a bra, but I didn't wear it often, especially in the summer when it was hot and uncomfortable. But if my breasts got much bigger, I'd have to start wearing it.

I wondered what it would feel like if someone else's hands were caressing my breasts. Someone I loved, someone warm. I ran my hands down my stomach and played with my bellybutton. I craned my neck to try to look into it, but I couldn't see very well. I rested my hands at the top of my jeans. I breathed deeply, in and out, letting my hands rise and fall with my stomach. There was still so much I had to learn about sex and love and myself. I figured it would come with time. But for now all I could do was just keep going.

Bear ran into my room, jumped on the bed, and gave me a sloppy dog kiss. I laughed, rubbed his belly, and nuzzled my face in his fur. He went over to Fred's cage, and Fred slipped into his shell, hiding yet again.

I stood up and examined myself in the mirror. My hair

had grown long enough to tuck behind my ears. I stared into my eyes—"such an unusual green"—and tried to catch myself not looking, which is virtually impossible to do in a mirror.

In my mind I heard Melita's voice calling me beautiful. I said my name, drawing out each syllable and exaggerating my lips as I formed the word. "Phoe-be." I puckered my lips and blew a kiss to my reflection. "You're pretty." I smiled because I believed it. I thought of my mother and wondered how I was like her and how I was like my own self. I made up my mind to ask Dad more about her. I wanted to know as much as possible. As much as he was willing to share. I could always ask Gerelyn, too. Between the two of them I might get a glimpse into her life.

I opened my box of photographs. When I got back from New York the week before, Dad surprised me by paying for my rolls of film to be developed. I sifted through them now. So much of my life documented. I started with the animals, still among my favorites, then some of Melita on the farm, and then went through the New York ones, taken with my new camera. People going about their regular lives with the buildings and the city behind them. Melita and Gerelyn with their arms wrapped around each other. You could tell they loved each other, even if they had a hard time sometimes. I got to the ones of Tomas playing his guitar. I had almost thrown them away, but then decided not to. Life is too fragile to throw people away. People are what make life interesting.

And then there were a couple that Melita had taken of me. They weren't bad, though it was obvious that I was uncomfortable. It was true, I was much happier behind the camera than in front of it.

The ones of the show had come out pretty well. When Dad first saw them, he was shocked to see all of my mother's clothes. He was all set to explode, but when I explained to him what we had done and why, he calmed down and said, "Well, I guess it's about time that stuff was used as it was intended. I don't know why I'm hanging on to it and keeping it in a box." Even my father can change sometimes.

I selected some of my favorites of Petunia and the sheep, even though they weren't as good quality. They seemed the most appropriate. Then I added a few of New York. They made an interesting contrast.

I stood by the phone and fingered the piece of paper with Beth's number on it, hesitating a minute, and then I dialed.

"Hello?" she answered.

"Beth? This is Phoebe. Phoebe Sharp?"

"Hey, hi! I'm so glad you called back." She sounded very chipper and a little nervous. "I'm getting ready to put the first paper out. Do you have some photos I could use? I was thinking something arty, maybe some of where you live. You'll get full credit, of course."

"I have some that might work," I said. I told her about the ones I'd picked out.

"Those sound great," she said. "A little bit of country and a little bit of city."

There was a pause and then Beth said, "Your friend that I met this summer, she's very hip."

"Melita," I said. "Yah, she is."

"Is she going to be in school with us?"

"No. She went back to New York." I told her about visiting New York and some of the things we did. I remembered how Melita had said Beth seemed like the most interesting person in town. "You'd like Melita," I added.

"She had cool hair," Beth said, then paused for a second. "Did you like New York?"

"Yes," I said. "I might go there for college to study photography or maybe film." I hadn't thought of that before, but as I said it I realized it could be true. I had to get to high school first, but maybe leaving Plattville wouldn't be so bad. There was so much else to experience, so many places to go. I could always come back. Plattville would always be there. I told Beth about the photography show I saw.

"That sounds really cool. I'd love to see something like that. I'm thinking of writing an article on the oldest living person in Plattville. Margie Appleby just turned one hundred. Maybe we could collaborate. I'll write and you can take the pictures."

I nodded and smiled even though Beth couldn't see me. Maybe Plattville was an exotic far-off land in its own right. "That sounds fun," I said.

"Really?" she asked.

"Sure."

"Because it was just an idea. We can do something else if you want, or nothing. I mean, you don't have to."

"No, I'd really like to, Beth."

"Great. That's great. Then I guess we'll have to spend some time together."

I nodded again. That wouldn't be so bad. Beth seemed like someone I could spend time with. "Okay," I said.

We went on, chatting easily. It turns out she is an avid reader, too, so we talked a lot about books we'd read and wanted to read. We talked about starting at the new consolidated school.

"It's bigger," Beth said. "We won't be as limited in who we can be friends with, you know? It'll be so much better."

"Yah, maybe," I said. Truth is, I hadn't given much thought to starting a new school. School was school.

"Phoebe?" she said.

"Yah?"

"I really am glad that you called back."

"Me, too," I said.

"I wasn't sure you would. You've always been so much cooler than everyone, you know? And a little distant. But when I saw you this summer, you seemed more approachable."

I had no idea what she was talking about. Me? Cool and unapproachable?

"Maybe when school starts we can hang out? I mean besides working on the article. Go to the library or something."

"Okay," I said.

"Do you like movies? We could rent a movie sometime."

"I'd like that," I said.

When we finally hung up, I'm sure I had the goofiest grin on my face. Maybe school wouldn't be so bad after all. Maybe there was life beyond unrequited love and being confused. Beth seemed like someone I could really talk to. I was already excited to show her my photographs.

Dad came in. "You look happy," he said.

"I'm going to have some of my photographs in the school paper," I said.

"Good for you, Phoebe!" He put his hand on my shoulder.

"Dad," I said, feeling confident, "will you tell me more about Mom? What she was like? I hardly know anything about her."

Dad pondered this and rubbed his beard, then slowly nodded. "You're right, Phoebe. It's about time you knew more. I've been wrong to keep everything from you. It's just that it still hurts after all this time. But you have a right to know. You are so much like her. Strong and determined and beautiful."

"Thanks, Dad." I felt a little embarrassed but happy at the same time.

"Tomorrow, I promise. You and I will sit down, just the two of us, and I'll tell you anything you want to know."

I threw my arms around him, and we stayed like that, in a real hug, for a full minute.

When I got ready for bed that night, the nip in the air made it chilly enough for me to wear my flannel pajamas. As I searched through my bottom drawer, I came across Lambchops's tail. I had washed it out a while ago so that

I could use it as a lucky sheep's tail. I rubbed it across my cheek. I remembered how Melita had been so nervous that day, it was almost comical.

So much had happened that summer. I knew myself better than I thought I did and it all made sense. Sometimes I was slow in figuring things out, but when the time was right, I could tell people how I felt and the world would not cave in around me and swallow me up. I had made one friend and I felt intense joy at the possibility of making another. No one could ever replace Melita. She was my best friend. My princess charming. Although I would not be carried off into a sunset of happily ever after. That happened only in fairy tales. But her kiss had woken me up and changed my life, at least for the time being, and that's all I can ever really know.